PRAISE FOR THE NOVELS OF

Kay Hooper

BL[...]

"You won't wan[...] [...]ng
this book!" —R[...]

"A good read for fans of other serial-killer [...] and
the TV show *Criminal Minds*." —*Booklist*

SLEEPING WITH FEAR

"An entertaining book for any reader."
—*Winston-Salem Journal*

"Hooper keeps the suspense dialed up.... Readers
will be mesmerized by a plot that moves quickly to a
chilling conclusion." —*Publishers Weekly*

CHILL OF FEAR

"Hooper's latest may offer her fans a few shivers on a
hot beach." —*Publishers Weekly*

"Kay Hooper has conjured a fine thriller with appeal-
ing young ghosts and a suitably evil presence to pro-
vide a welcome chill on a hot summer's day."
—*Orlando Sentinel*

"The author draws the reader into the story line and, once there, they can't leave because they want to see what happens next in this thrill-a-minute, chilling, fantastic reading experience." —*Midwest Book Review*

HUNTING FEAR

"A well-told scary story." —*Toronto Sun*

"Hooper's unerring story sense and ability to keep the pages flying can't be denied."
—*Ellery Queen's Mystery Magazine*

"Hooper has created another original—*Hunting Fear* sets an intense pace.... Work your way through the terror to the triumph...and you'll be looking for more Hooper tales to add to your bookshelf."
—Wichita Falls *Times Record News*

"It's vintage Hooper—a suspenseful page-turner."
—Brazosport *Facts*

"Expect plenty of twists and surprises as Kay Hooper gets her series off to a crackerjack start!"
—*Aptos Times*

SENSE OF EVIL

"A well-written, entertaining police procedural... loaded with suspense."
—*Midwest Book Review*

KAY HOOPER

~

Larger than Life

BANTAM BOOKS

2009 Bantam Books Mass Market Edition

Published in the United States by Bantam Books, an imprint of
The Random House Publishing Group, a division of Random
House, Inc., New York.

BANTAM BOOKS and the rooster colophon are registered
trademarks of Random House, Inc.

Originally published in mass market in the United States by
Bantam Books, an imprint of The Random House Publishing
Group, a division of Random House, Inc., in 1986.

ISBN: 978-0-553-59057-9

Cover design: Yook Louie

Printed in the United States of America

www.bantamdell.com

9 8 7 6 5 4 3 2 1

For Linda

Larger
than Life

PROLOGUE

SHE ADJUSTED THE straps of the backpack absently and stared at the glass doors leading into the terminal. For a fleeting moment, she wanted badly to take a ship instead of a plane, but stoically she controlled her fear.

Squaring her shoulders, she walked forward. Just inside the terminal was a tall man. He detached himself from the crowd he blended with so well and fell quietly and smoothly into step beside her.

"Matt wants to see you."

She smiled wryly to herself as she halted and stood scanning the arrival and departure monitors. "I want to see him, too."

"The jet's this way."

They walked side by side through the busy terminal: a small, slight young woman dressed in faded jeans and a workshirt and a tall but otherwise undistinguished-looking middle-aged man who was dressed casually but with an indefinable air of affluence.

"You're looking well, Alex," she said.

"So are you."

If there was any censure in his calm, level voice, only the girl's sharp and experienced ears could have detected it. And she did detect it, for she grimaced faintly. She said nothing as they left the building and crossed the tarmac toward a gleaming Lear jet.

Then, suddenly, she said, "The credit card in Wanganui."

Her companion had no apparent difficulty in deciphering this cryptic statement. "You purchased some clothing and a backpack, and told the shopkeeper you were heading for Auckland. We've been here for three weeks."

She nodded slightly. "A mistake on my part, but I didn't have any cash."

"Fortunately for Matt."

She made no answer to that but climbed aboard the jet. She nodded to the pilot and copilot, both familiar faces; slung her backpack onto an extra chair in the luxurious cabin, and silently strapped herself into her seat. Alex just as silently followed suit as the pilots went forward to the cockpit.

"Why didn't you call Matt?"

"At first because I couldn't." She gazed out the window, no expression on her lovely face. "Later ... well, I don't know why I didn't call him later."

"He's been half out of his mind."

"I don't need you to tell me that."

He was silent for a moment. "You've changed."

"Have I?" She thought about that for a while, her hands gripping the armrests rather fiercely as the jet lifted into the air; that one sign of tension disappeared, though, when the aircraft had leveled off. Then she smiled and murmured as if to herself. "I didn't change."

He looked at her quickly, sharply. And what he saw disquieted him, almost unnerved him. She had always seemed to him a flower, lovely and fragile, with no ability to live outside the pampered world so lovingly provided for her. He wondered what Matt was going to make of her. Sun-browned and reed slim, she was no longer the delicate creature her life had made her. Her step held the springiness of strong muscles, her movements the unthinking grace of a dancer or athlete. There was cool self-possession in her lovely face and restless energy in her silver-gray eyes. Even her voice had changed from soft and sweet to low and husky.

Finally he said, "We'll be home soon."

She gave him an unreadable look. "Will we?"

There didn't seem to be anything he could say to that.

ONE

SHE WAS EXTRAORDINARY. Compelling. Exquisite.
Waves of smoldering sensuality emanated from her
striking silvery eyes and slender body to hold the
audience spellbound. Her sequined gown was a
shimmering silver, molding to her like a second
skin: the bare flesh it revealed was tanned a smooth
gold. Her thick, shining ebony hair hung about her
shoulders in a living curtain of darkness. And her
voice . . . throaty, sensual, filled with an odd defiant
yearning, endowing the words of the song with a

wild plea that touched every person in the audience. Women, old and young alike, felt their throats constrict and eyes fill with tears as the passionate words seemed to rise from their own deepest selves. And men of all ages felt their hearts thudding dully in their ears, conscious of a desperate desire to go out and slay dragons. . . .

The man standing in the wings felt the compulsion toward heroic deeds, felt his heart pounding fiercely. A distant part of his mind marveled silently at the effect of the woman and the woman's voice. In little less than a year, she'd won over popular music fans throughout the country. The world, her manager had mentioned casually, happily, was next.

Travis Foxx, standing next to that manager now was conscious of a dozen questions he wanted to ask. But he listened, instead, to a voice rich with a woman's passion and to words that stripped that woman's soul naked as she sang of the dearth of heroes.

"Isn't she something?" Philip Saunders asked cheerfully, clearly expecting a positive response.

Travis reluctantly pulled his gaze from the stage as Saber Duncan instantly went into another song, barely giving the stunned audience time to applaud. "Yes. Yes, she's certainly something." Travis's resonant voice added coolly, "But is she the same woman who released a couple of—in all honesty—forgettable songs just about two years ago?"

Saunders blinked, then laughed. "You've heard the rumors, I see."

"That perhaps she isn't Saber Duncan at all, but a ringer brought in by Mosaic Records? I've heard. And now I wonder." With an effort Travis closed his ears to that enchanting voice scant feet away, focusing his attention on the man at his side. "I heard those forgettable songs when the records were released. And that voice wasn't the one I'm hearing tonight."

"You're so sure of that?"

Travis ignored the mild question. "That voice was as sweet as honey and just as bland. No power. Certainly no passion. And I have copies of the studio photos released to the press then. That Saber was a girl, a hothouse flower with the dew still on its petals."

"Nice imagery," Saunders murmured, clearly amused.

He was ignored again. "*This* Saber"—Travis gestured toward the performer onstage—"is part jungle cat and part siren. And her voice holds more power, more raw passion, then I've heard from a performer in fifteen years." He lifted an eyebrow at the smiling manager. "Such a change in a single year? Sorry, Saunders, but I'm having a hard time swallowing that."

"Hence the book?" Saunders questioned dryly.

Travis turned his gaze back to the stage, his eyes drawn like a lodestone to the woman pouring her heart out so compellingly. "That's partly the reason," he answered honestly. "I've never written a biography before, as I told you...."

"But you want to write hers." Saunders filled in the sudden silence between them with wry words. "Well, I warned you. Saber's a very, very private person. I honestly think she'll refuse to authorize you to write about her."

Shifting his weight restlessly in an unconscious movement, Travis frowned, not noticing the thoughtful gaze of the other man. "I'll talk her into it. There isn't enough material for a single chapter in that scanty bio you release to the press; I haven't been able to build a profile on her." His frowning eyes returned to the manager's expressionless face. "One thing I have been able to find out: Saber Duncan was born just about two years ago. The bio that Mosaic—or you, or she—concocted is just that. Concocted."

Philip Saunders was silent for a long moment, his level hazel eyes weighing, considering. Then he sighed. Softly he quoted, " 'You would pluck out the heart of my mystery; you would sound me from my lowest note to the top of my compass.' "

It was Travis's turn to blink. "Shakespeare. *Hamlet.*" He identified the quote easily, then the words sank in. Before he could comment, Saunders was explaining.

"That's something Saber quoted to me about a year ago, when I signed on to manage her career. When—not to put too fine a point on it—I was asking a few questions about her life before I entered it."

Travis was more than a little surprised, and slightly suspicious. "Are you trying to tell me that you're no better informed about her than the public?"

Saunders was unoffended. "That's what I'm telling you. Oh, if you want to write that high-quality stuff, like what she eats for dinner or what her favorite colors are, I could probably oblige. But if you want the sordid details of her shady past—"

Travis cut him off with an impatient gesture. "I don't want to write a damned 'Meet the Latest Superstar' book, whether you believe that or not."

"Oh, I believe it." Saunders's voice was abruptly sober. "I've read some of your stuff, Mr. Foxx. You write exceptionally strong fiction and stunning nonfictional exposés. Your books hit the bestseller lists as soon as they land in the bookstores."

Travis's green eyes sharpened. "But you don't want me probing into your client's background?"

"*She* doesn't want it. And that's good enough for me. Look, Foxx, there's almost a year missing from Saber's professional life. And, as you pointed out, that professional life covers only a scant two years. She cut two quick singles, vanished for months, then reappeared and, virtually overnight, became a star." He folded his arms across his chest and stared broodingly at the other man. "Now I don't know where she was during those missing months, but I'm reasonably certain she went through hell; I've seen the studio pics and heard the 'forgettable' songs, too, you see."

"And you aren't curious?"

"That's a mild word. Let's set my 'curiosity' aside for the moment, shall we? The facts and obligations are clear. Saber's my client; I handle her professional commitments and try to protect her from harm. Tonight marks the tenth city of a twelve-city tour, and I'm going to see to it that my client takes a nice long rest just as soon as this tour's over. Saber's also my friend: she's tired—and I worry about her. I worry because that incredible energy she manifests onstage is an illusion at best and a shield at worst. Offstage she cages that jungle-cat wildness you mentioned and hides behind the bars.

She's no hothouse flower, but she's vulnerable. And I won't have her hurt."

"You're so sure I'd hurt her?"

"If you dig up a past she wants—for whatever reason—to remain buried, yes, you'll hurt her."

Travis turned his gaze back to the stage, where Saber Duncan was winding up her performance. "I want to talk to her," he said.

"I'll introduce you." Saunders responded non-committally.

Thunderous applause followed her as Saber left the stage. She handed her microphone to a grinning stagehand and turned to the two men waiting in the wings.

Saunders stepped forward. "Saber, this is Travis Foxx," he said.

"Miss Duncan." He was momentarily surprised by the firm strength of her slender fingers as they shook hands; then she looked at him, and the fascination of her odd silver eyes drove all else from his mind.

"Hi," she said softly.

Travis plunged in headfirst. "I'd like to talk to

you, Miss Duncan, whenever it's convenient." She was a tiny woman, he realized bemusedly; oddly, she'd looked so much larger onstage.

The silver eyes were gazing up at him without expression. "Sorry, Mr. Foxx, but I'm leaving the city tomorrow morning."

"My travel plans are flexible," he said.

"I don't like interviews." Her voice was still soft.

"I'm not a reporter, Miss Duncan. I want to write a book—"

"I know. I'm not interested, Mr. Foxx."

"How can you be sure until you hear what I've got to say?"

"I am sure. Sorry. Phil, there are some things we have to go over before I leave. How about a late dinner?"

"You're on."

She looked back at Travis. "Mr. Foxx, I *am* sorry. It's a shame you had to come all this way for nothing. Please try to understand. I just don't want a book written about me." She smiled, a shadow of the blinding onstage grin, but curiously more real and infinitely sweeter. "It was nice meeting you." Then she took her manager's arm and vanished down the corridor to the dressing rooms.

Travis stood still for a long moment, listening without really hearing the muted roar of the departing audience. He wasn't particularly disappointed by Saber's refusal; in fact, he had expected her to refuse. But he'd hardly become known as a brilliant journalistic writer by giving up whenever a subject refused to confide in him.

So rather than wasting energy in being irritated, he thought carefully instead. He thought about where Saber and her manager would likely go for a late dinner. Then he turned on his heel and hurried toward the stage door.

As he'd expected, his subject returned to her hotel to dine, where the late night quiet and relative dimness of the restaurant lessened the odds of her being recognized. Watching them from across the room as he finished his own meal, Travis noted that she'd changed into slacks and a silk blouse but had not chosen to sport sunglasses, a hat, or any of the other traditional—and usually ridiculous—trappings of disguise.

His chance came when the pair he watched had reached the coffee stage of their meal and Saunders left the table with an audible request to his client to please get some rest before her morning flight. Grabbing his opportunity, Travis rose quickly and crossed to her table, where she was going over sheet music.

"May I join you?" he asked, sliding into a chair.

She gazed at him for a long moment, a look of irony in her silver-gray eyes. "Oh, please do," she invited gently.

"I hate rudeness in strangers, don't you?" he said conversationally.

"It's trying," she agreed.

"And it's so hard to get rid of the determined ones, I find."

She sighed. "Mr. Foxx—"

"Travis, please."

Giving him another of those direct, ironic looks, she sighed again. "Travis, you have what I can see is a well-deserved reputation for tenacity. I can admire that. In fact, I'm that way myself. But to even the most tenacious eventually comes something that's...out of reach."

"In your experience?" he inquired politely.

"A truth of life, let's say."

"Saber— You don't mind if I call you that, do you?"

"Strangers do," she murmured.

He couldn't help but smile at her left-handed acceptance. "Saber, I adhere to another truth of life."

"I'm going to hate myself for asking, but what's that?"

" 'He can who believes he can.' I learned that at my father's knee."

Saber sat back, smiling a little. "From what I've read, your father nearly invented that philosophy. He was a self-made man, wasn't he? Built a knowledge of electronics into a world-renowned firm?"

"He did indeed."

"You chose not to follow in his footsteps?"

"I prefer writing. My brother runs the firm."

"I didn't realize you had a brother. Other siblings?"

"Two sisters..."

Later, Travis realized with something between shock and amusement that he'd allowed himself to become the interviewee rather than the interviewer. And the amusement in those silvery eyes revealed that she had deliberately planned to turn the tables on him. She now knew far more about his life and past than he knew about hers.

"Very good," he noted dryly with a small salute.

"Thank you."

"I don't suppose you'd consider a fair trade of information?"

"I don't think so."

Travis's hunting instincts were now fully roused. He studied her keenly across the table. "Mind if I make a few guesses?"

"Go right ahead."

He sat back, mentally processing what very few observations and impressions he'd been able to acquire. "And just out of a sense of fair play, you understand, would you correct me if I go too far off base?" He was banking on her lack of concern over what he might guess, trusting in the inevitable human leaning toward complacency.

After a moment, she nodded slowly. "All right, Travis. If any of your guesses is glaringly wrong, I'll point that out."

Mere recognition of wrongness rather than correction was not quite what he'd hoped for, but he settled for it. Gathering his thoughts, he began.

"Saber Duncan is not the name you were born with. You've led—up until two years ago, at any rate—a very sheltered life. You're very well educated, partly outside this country, I think. And two years ago, shortly after you cut your first two records, something happened to you, something that changed your voice, your style...even your life. Right so far?"

She was smiling faintly. "Not glaringly wrong."

He took a deep breath and began calling forth more personal observations and perceptions. "I don't know what happened to you during those missing months, Saber, but I'm sure it was devastating in some way. Because the lovely, fragile hot-

house flower with the sweet, passionless voice became something—someone—far more compli-
cated. I think you walked through fire."

There was something now behind the serenity of
her eyes, a glimpse of that part of her she kept
caged offstage. But she was still smiling. " 'I am
ashes where once I was fire'?" she murmured.

He shook his head, staring into her eyes as he
tried to find and catch that elusive wildness behind
the silvery curtain. "No. You're fire now...where
once you were something cool and dry."

"And that's what interests you, isn't it?"
Abruptly, she was distant, matter-of-fact. "What
happened to the girl who became a woman? What
happened to a hothouse flower to make it grow in
the harsh outdoors? That's why you're hell-bent
to write a book about me. Not because of who
and what I've become, but because you don't
know how that happened, and you hate unsolved
mysteries."

Travis gazed at her for a long moment. He could
hardly deny the quiet accusation, because it was
true. But he realized now that the man was as

intrigued by her as the writer. "Will you answer one question honestly?" he asked at last.

"I'll have to hear it first."

He nodded, expecting nothing else. "Are you the Saber Duncan who recorded two records two years ago?"

"Yes."

"If you'd answered no," he said quietly, "I would have lost the desire to write about you. Because you're quite right: what fascinates me isn't that you're a 'star' or even that now you have the most incredible voice I've ever heard. It's that two years ago you were a girl with a sweet, bland voice, and now you're a woman whose larger-than-life stage presence is matched by something I sense in you offstage. Something equally larger than life."

"That's honest, anyway." Her voice was curiously husky.

He leaned forward intently. "I write about *people,* Saber. Fictional characters or factual lives—but always people. What motivates them, what drives them. *How* they've become what they are. In a way, it's like that song of yours. There are so few larger-than-life people, so few heroes and heroines. I write about the people who become heroic."

"I'm not heroic."

"One of the definitions of *heroic* is *larger than life*." he said softly. "And you are that, Saber."

She shook her head, denying the words or any reference to herself in them.

After a moment, he said, "I can promise that you will have final approval of the manuscript. I won't allow anything to get into print that you don't want in print."

"Then you'd have no book," she said quietly. "Because what I don't want in print... is most of my life."

TWO

THE SILENCE STRETCHED between them for long moments. Then Travis spoke slowly and thoughtfully.

"The past—anyone's past—is important only in that it shaped the present. Can you accept that I need to know about your past in order to understand your present?"

"I certainly can. I just can't accept the necessity of seeing my past in print."

"It doesn't have to be seen in print. As long as I

understand what's gone before, I can put the present into perspective."

"No. Not my present."

"Because without your past, there isn't a present?"

She smiled slightly and gently shook her head. "Travis, try to understand how I feel about this. Certain . . . events in my life over which I had little or no control shaped me into who and what I am. We could get into a long discussion over the importance of pasts, but right now, in this moment of my present, I'm very tired. And my past doesn't seem important to *me,* much less to the world."

"You avoided answering my question," he said softly.

She sighed. "I suppose I did. I'm not quite up to your weight tonight, I'm afraid. So I think I'd better go up to my room; I have an early plane tomorrow."

He rose to his feet as she did. "I'm not giving up."

"I wonder why that doesn't surprise me," she said dryly.

It wasn't difficult to discover what Saber's travel plans were—not, at least, for a man experienced in unearthing information. In fact, by ten the next morning, Travis knew that Saber's band members were on a commercial flight to Detroit, her manager on one to Los Angeles. He knew that Saunders was cutting short his participation in the tour with two performances left to go because of business appointments in L.A. And he knew that Saber would fly to Detroit in a small private jet.

It was a bit more difficult to get himself aboard that jet before she arrived, but he managed, conscious of his own wry amusement at what he was doing. He had realized during the night that his interest in Saber was no longer purely literary, but he was more than a little surprised to discover that his growing fascination was almost wholly due to her eyes. Or, more correct, what shone in her eyes. Beneath the silver-gray serenity of her gaze lay something else, something that had reminded Travis irresistibly of a wild thing crouched in waiting behind iron bars. There were secrets imprisoned behind those cool, serene eyes, secrets and a powerful but elusive part of her that Travis suspected had been born during the year of her disappearance. He was positive that the published accounts of her life up until she'd begun singing were wholly fictional, but of that missing year not even a *fictional* report had been given. Saber the performer had ceased to exist; Saber the woman, he felt intuitively, had walked through some kind of metaphorical fire.

He meant to find out exactly what had happened. And he was bemused to discover that his professional interest in that question had become very personal indeed.

He shelved that thought for the time being as he slipped aboard the jet and hid himself in the tiny bathroom. His patient wait consumed three-quarters of an hour before he heard Saber's low, cheerful voice speaking to someone else. He listened to the noises of the jet's engines and of the door being closed. The jet taxied for a bit, paused, then taxied again before increasing speed and lifting from the runway.

Travis waited until the aircraft had leveled off before he quit his hiding place. Out in the cabin, however, he experienced a considerable shock. It was empty. No Saber. No anybody else. If she wasn't here...Frowning, he gazed toward the closed door leading to the cockpit.

When he opened the door and squeezed his way inside, he found Saber Duncan alone and at the controls.

She swung her head around to stare up at him, surprise widening the silvery eyes. "What're you doing here?" she asked.

"I think it's called stowing away." Gingerly, he took the copilot's seat, careful to touch nothing. "And I'd appreciate it if you kept both eyes on the road."

Saber turned her attention forward again and, to his surprise, laughed quietly. "Well, I'll say this for you: you don't give up easily."

Travis studied her for a long moment. Gone was the sequined, explosively powerful performer of the night before. Gone was the soft-spoken and somewhat weary lady of the silk blouse and veiled eyes. This lady was casually dressed in jeans and a workshirt open over a cowl-neck sweater, her tiny feet encased in scuffed western boots. The only jewelry she wore was a broad, masculine watch on her left wrist, and her delicate golden face was bare of any makeup.

She looked amazingly small, incredibly young, and as frail as the hothouse flower he'd compared the earlier Saber to. Yet there was something about her, something he sensed more than saw.

"You'll know me if we ever meet again," she said dryly.

Travis blinked and forced his mind away from the speculation. "Sorry. It's just that...you seem so different."

She obviously had no trouble following his vague comment. "From the stage performance, you mean? That's because I am different. Every performer has two sides, one for the stage and one for the personal life. We can't be 'on' all the time, you know."

He frowned a little, listening to the soft, educated voice, the crisp, clean tone. "I know that. But you aren't . . . 'off' now. You're just different."

Her light eyes moved ceaselessly over the instrument panels and her small hands gripped the controls a little too firmly. "Does it matter?"

Travis noted the signs of tension and made a surprising discovery. "You're afraid of something, aren't you?"

She threw him one startled look and then returned her attention to the controls, making an odd little grimace. "Very perceptive of you. And since," she added wryly, "I'm not particularly concerned with the nerves of my stowaway, I'll confess that what I'm afraid of, Travis, is flying."

"You're afraid of flying?"

"That's right. Almost a phobia, in fact."

"Then what the hell are you doing flying this jet?" he demanded incredulously.

"A very wise man told me once that a person should always try to control fear. And since the only way I can control my fear of flying is by doing the thing myself, that's what I do. I *am* a licensed pilot. I learned to fly years ago. I'm fairly new to jets, though."

"Great." But in spite of his doubtful tone, Travis was impressed by her method of handling fear. It told him a great deal about her personality; she was one who would always confront a problem head-on and set about solving it. And his silent observation was proven when she took her present problem by the horns.

"I told you I didn't want a book written about me, Travis. I haven't changed my mind."

"And I haven't given up."

"Obviously."

"All I'm asking," he said with persuasive charm, "is a chance to get to know you, Saber. No probing questions, I promise. I just want to get better acquainted with a very beautiful and talented woman."

"D'you generally get results with that line?"

So much for my vaunted charm, he thought, not without a trace of self-mockery. "Sorry," he muttered. "I didn't mean to try, uh—"

"You have a very effective voice," she observed.

"Just the right blend of coolness and charm. I'm not surprised your exposés are so penetrating; it would be very easy for your victim to forget that you're always after some little tidbit of information."

He stiffened, then relaxed suddenly. "But not this *victim*?" he drawled.

She was smiling, though still not looking at him. "No, not this one. You can save your subtly probing tactics, Travis, for your next exposé. My life is my business. I accept that my profession puts me in the public eye, but I see no need of sharing my life before I stepped onstage. You go ahead and write an unauthorized version of my life," she added imperturbably.

"And what'll you do if I uncover the real story of your life?"

"You won't."

"You're so sure?"

"Quite sure. I'm not throwing down the gauntlet, you understand; I'm simply stating a fact. You won't find out anything I don't want you to know."

After a moment, Travis said softly, "That kind of cover-up demands money."

She was mildly surprised. "Did I mention a cover-up?"

"That's what it amounts to."

"Not at all. You just won't know where to look, that's all."

"I know where I'll start."

"Oh? Where?"

"With the lady herself."

"In case you've forgotten," she said politely, "I happen to be on rather a tight schedule. A performance in Detroit tonight, then one in Chicago tomorrow night."

"Then a vacation."

Saber threw him one quick glance, annoyance warring with reluctant amusement in her light eyes. "So you know that, do you? Phil must have let that slip."

"Yes. To do him justice, I don't think he realized just how determined I am."

"Well, be that as it may, the information won't help you."

"Really? I find most information useful—eventually."

She was quiet for a long moment. Then, in a curiously dry voice, she said, "Short of pushing you out, I can't stop you from coming to Detroit. And though I'll take good care you don't board this jet again, I can't stop you from taking a commercial plane to Chicago. But from that point, Mr. Foxx, you'll be at a standstill. My flight plan will be filed, of course, but—for security reasons, you understand—you won't be able to find out where I've gone. If you're a betting man, bet on that."

Travis was well aware of the dangers of arguing with a woman who literally held his life in her hands, but the cool and certain strength of her voice intrigued him past the point of worrying about it. He gazed forward for several minutes, his keen mind working. The struggle he had with himself was brief, then his idea for the book was cast into the limbo of things unremembered and unregretted.

"I am a betting man," he said finally. "In fact, I'm a bit of a gambler, and when I want something badly enough, I'm quite prepared to pay the price."

"And so?" She sent him a curious glance.

"And so... I'll make a deal with you, Miss Duncan."

"I've a feeling I'm going to regret this—but what kind of deal?"

"Something for something. You agree to allow me to accompany you until, say, midway through your vacation. In the interests of our getting to know each other, you understand."

Noncommittally, she said, "And your part of the deal?"

"I'll agree—in writing if you like—to write nothing about you. No book, no article... nothing at all."

Saber was frowning. "There's a hook in there somewhere," she said.

"Not at all. I'll promise not to write about you if you'll promise to let us get to know each other... without prejudice."

"Why?"

"Why what?"

"Why would you give up your idea for a book that has been your driving motivation to this point just for a couple of weeks in my company?"

"Because you were right about me. I hate unsolved mysteries. What the public does or doesn't know about you doesn't particularly concern me, but I very badly want to understand you."

She was still frowning. "Why?" she asked again.

"Because...you fascinate me," he answered, turning his head to study her profile. "Maybe it's that larger-than-life part of you—"

"Stage presence," she dismissed impatiently.

"No. No, there's more to it than that. Saber, you wouldn't believe me if I explained what I'm feeling, and I'm no more anxious than any other man to look like a fool. So you'll just have to accept that I want to get to know you. Period."

For the first time, Saber's attention to piloting the jet was only automatic; she was entirely caught up with what Travis was saying. After a long moment, she said, "Maybe you'd better define your idea of 'accompanying' me for a couple of weeks."

Bluntly, he said, "I'm not asking you to sleep

with me to avoid my writing the book. No strings, Saber. The only promise I demand is that you treat me as you would any man who was interested in you as a woman. The only promise I'll give is that I won't write about you."

As blunt as he, she asked, "You're trying to tell me you're attracted to me? That's why you're willing to give up the book idea?"

Amused at her dispensing with the euphemistic niceties, he nodded. "That can't surprise you, surely?"

Saber, with a year of superstardom behind her and twenty-five years before that of male attention, wasn't surprised; men found her attractive, and she would have had to be blind not to know that. But to say that she distrusted Travis Foxx's professed admiration of her would have been a gross understatement.

"I don't trust you," she said matter-of-factly.

Travis chuckled. "I know that. But you have a choice, Saber. You can refuse my terms, which will only make me very determined to find out what I can about your mysterious past—and I think it only fair to warn you that I have sources of information you wouldn't think possible. Or you can accept my terms, thereby keeping your past hidden as long as you want."

Saber was smiling now. "I wonder," she said thoughtfully, "if you're counting on the well-known feminine response to a challenge. Which are you hoping for? That I'll dare you to uncover my sordid past? Or that I'll invite your wonderfully *uninquisitive* self into my life—however temporarily?"

"Touché," he replied, laughing. "You're a very sharp lady, Miss Duncan. We both know I plan to get my answers by whichever path. So it's up to you."

"Isn't it, though." Her tone was dry.

Sobering, Travis said, "In all honesty, I'd rather spend time with you than spend time researching you. And in the former case, you have the satisfaction of knowing that your past will remain hidden to the public."

"You're very sure you can . . . persuade me to tell you all about myself, aren't you, Travis?"

"Quite sure," he said coolly.

Her smile widened. "I wonder which of us is more stubborn," she murmured.

"Shall we find out?"

Saber was not a reckless woman, but the challenge in this man's green eyes was impossible to ignore. "Let's," she said suddenly, briskly. "And devil take the hindmost."

Travis smiled and nodded. That the lady looked upon this as a challenging game was obvious; that his own motives in playing were quite serious was something he had no intention of trying to persuade her at this early stage.

An expert sportsman, Travis was hunting this time with more than a story at stake. Much more.

The Detroit performance went off without a hitch, as Travis was privileged to see from the wings. Saber had treated him casually and companionably all day, allowing him to watch the rehearsal and take her to lunch. She'd seemed not the least bit on guard, but Travis had realized that her serene silver-gray eyes were shields in and of themselves.

As for himself, he shelved questions about the past and simply absorbed the present. He noted that the members of Saber's band treated her with affection and respect. The feeling of family was unmistakable and, for Travis, significant, considering that these people lived in the fast-paced and—as far as the public was concerned—decadent world of popular music. They were also quite protective of her: more than one suspicious eye had been cast at him when she'd casually introduced him.

Travis met suspicion with blandness and watched quietly from the sidelines studying Saber's professionalism and marveling at her talent. He didn't attempt to flatter her but acknowledged to himself that her manager had been quite right in his belief that the world would fall at her feet.

After a late and somewhat quiet dinner at their hotel, Travis left her at the door to her room. And when the Lear departed Detroit the next morning, he was beside her in the cockpit.

The day in Chicago went pretty much as the day

before, with rehearsals and a flawless performance, then a late dinner and polite good-nights.

It didn't occur to Travis until then that he didn't know where "they" were going on Saber's vacation. Nor did it occur to him that since he'd made no reservation at this hotel, a room couldn't be found for him. But so it was. Five separate conventions were being held in the hotel, and even the broom closets, the desk clerk assured him in a harassed voice, were occupied.

Silently berating himself for not having arranged things earlier in the day, Travis recovered his bag from the luggage room. Then, after a glance at his watch and a moment's thought, he headed for the elevator again. Five minutes later he was knocking on Saber's door.

After a moment, the night chain rattled and she pulled the door open, having obviously looked through the security peephole. "Hello," she said politely.

Intellectually, he realized there was nothing even remotely sexy about her nightgown. It was a flannel affair, high-necked and long-sleeved, deep blue in color and reaching down to her ankles. Still, curiously, Travis felt his toes curl inside his shoes and concentrated on straightening them out; he was so astonished at his own reaction that it was several long moments before he remembered why he was standing there.

Clearing his throat, he said, "You have a two-room suite. Right?"

"Right." She leaned against the doorjamb, gazing at him with elaborate politeness.

"Then would you mind very much if I borrowed your couch?" He assumed his best beaten-spaniel look. "The hotel doesn't have a closet to spare, and since it's past midnight..."

"Did you plan this?" she asked in a mildly interested voice.

"No, I swear."

She nodded and stepped back with a slight gesture. "You're welcome to the couch."

Her immediate acceptance surprised Travis somewhat, but when he'd followed her into the living room and placed his garment bag over a chair, he saw what he'd missed before: she was exhausted.

"I ordered some coffee," she said idly as she sat down at the table by the window. She picked up a cup from the tray in front of her. "There's another cup if you'd like some."

Travis crossed slowly to sit down in the chair across from hers, his eyes intent, concerned. "I'd say the last thing you needed was coffee."

She sipped the hot liquid, her faintly smiling eyes meeting his over the rim of her cup. "It helps me stay awake long enough to unwind," she said. "Otherwise I sleep, but I don't rest."

He realized abruptly what this tour must have cost her. Twelve performances, twelve cities, twelve days. Her face, bare of makeup, was so pale it looked translucent, the cool tautness now relaxed in weariness. The strength and power of her onstage and her cheerful energy offstage had deceived him into believing she was almost invincible.

Saber smiled a little beneath his scrutiny. "I look like a hag, huh?" she asked, her tone one of wry self-realization.

"You look—very tired."

"What nice manners you have, sir."

Travis ignored the gentle mockery. "Your manager ought to be shot for putting you through this kind of tour," he said flatly.

"Fair's fair. It was my idea; Phil tried to discourage me."

"Then you should be shot."

She shook her head. "A little tiredness is a small price to pay for the exposure."

He studied her thoughtfully. "Funny, but I get the impression you don't care a bit for your fame."

"I don't." She met his gaze, her own unwavering. "But I do care for my success."

"You're a star. You perform for sellout crowds; your records sell in the millions; you'll never be able to spend all the money you've made. What more is there to work for?"

Saber, more weary than she'd realized, answered without remembering that Travis was a man to be wary of. "Not more. Never less. I have to prove—" She broke off, vaguely aware of danger.

"Prove what?" he asked softly. "To whom?"

"Prove I can do it," she answered. "Prove to him I can make it—" For a moment, her tired gray eyes stared into his. Then a veil dropped. She set her cup down and rose to her feet. "I'm going to bed," she said distantly. "See you in the morning."

Travis, on his feet in an instant, reached out a hand to catch her wrist before she could turn away. "Saber, I'm sorry. You're too tired to think, and I had no business taking advantage of that." Honestly contrite, he was aware that his voice was anxious but was too worried over having unthinkingly probed to be concerned that he might be betraying himself.

She looked at him, a little puzzled, a little amused. "You're...a strange man, Travis," she said. "I can't quite figure you out."

He lifted his free hand to touch her cheek. "Then don't try," he urged softly. "Just accept that I...care about you." It was more than he'd meant to say, but she looked so tired and worn and he couldn't stop the words.

Conscious of the warmth of his hand against her skin, Saber was finding it difficult to think. She gazed up into green eyes that were warm and concerned and something else she couldn't identify, wondering dimly why the room had shrunk so that he seemed to fill it. He was taller than she'd realized, his eyes greener, his face more handsome.

Why hadn't she noticed that before now?

Travis stepped forward abruptly, his hand cradling the nape of her neck, his fingers tangling in her thick hair; he bent his head, and his lips found hers. He kissed her as if she were something infinitely precious and fragile, a tender kiss over almost before it began.

"Good night, Saber. Sleep well."

Silently, she turned to the bedroom. Closing the door behind her, she leaned against it for a moment. She needed to think, there was something very important she needed to think about, but her mind was blank. Vaguely she heard Travis on the phone requesting an extra pillow and blanket. She couldn't think about that, either. Sighing unconsciously, she got into bed and turned out the lamp on the nightstand. She was asleep almost instantly.

In the other room, Travis placed a second call,

this one to the harried hotel operator to ask if Saber had requested a wake-up call. Learning that she had placed one for eight A.M., he canceled it, representing himself as her manager. The operator, with a hotel full of merry conventioneers, accepted his authority without question.

Then Travis settled back to brood over the identity of the "him" Saber was so determined to prove herself to.

When he finally fell asleep, after lying awake long into the night, Travis slept hard. And he was considerably disgruntled when a hand shook his shoulder and ruthlessly yanked him from a pleasurable dream involving gray eyes and a ridiculously sexy blue flannel nightgown.

"Travis? *Travis.*"

Growling peevishly, he pulled his pillow around his ears to shut out the sadistic voice, groping mentally for his lost dream. Recapturing the image of gray eyes and blue nightgown, he soon became engrossed in the natural progression of things, only to sit bolt upright with a yelp, wide awake, when icy water was dumped unceremoniously on his face.

"What the hell!"

"Good morning," Saber offered sweetly. She stood gazing down at him, holding an empty glass in one hand and smiling without an ounce of compunction.

Travis wiped the water from his face and glared at her, automatically taking note of her jeans and sweater and of the fact that she was wide awake and seemingly well rested. "What's the big idea?" he demanded.

"When you sleep, you don't fool around, do you?"

"So you poured water on me?"

Saber waved the empty glass in a slight gesture. "Well, since I couldn't wake you up any other way, and since the brunch I ordered is due to arrive in about half an hour, I thought I'd try the water. Worked, too."

"Brunch?" he ventured, belatedly remembering where he was.

"Uh-huh. Oddly enough, I didn't get my wake-up call. It's now ten-thirty, and you have half an hour to make yourself presentable."

"I'm not presentable?"

"You have a morning stubble," she said.

Travis found himself grinning. "Not very diplomatic, are you?"

"The word is honest. If you want pretty speeches, you've got the wrong girl."

He cast aside his blanket and swung his long legs to the floor. "Funny, I dreamed I had the right one. She was wearing a ridiculous flannel night-gown and worshiped the ground I walked on."

"Fancy that. Must have been a lady of scanty intellect."

"You've already poured water on me; don't compound the felony."

She indicated the bathroom with a finger not wrapped around the glass. "Would you please go shave and put on something a bit more decent than those pajama bottoms?"

"Are they getting to you?" he asked with a mock leer.

"No," she replied, deadpan. "But one never knows how other people will react, and the waiter's coming, after all."

Travis sighed and held up a hand in surrender. "Uncle! From now on, I'll know better than to fence with you in the morning."

Saber inclined her head in gracious acknowledgment. She put the glass down and began folding the blanket as he gathered his things and disappeared into the bathroom. When he emerged some moments past the allotted time, he was shaved, showered, and dressed, and the door had just closed behind the departing waiter.

She greeted him with, "Hope you don't hate omelets," sounding as if she didn't much care whether he hated them or not.

"No," he said politely, taking his seat across from her at the table. "Love them, in fact."

Pouring their coffee, Saber sent him an amused look. "A question?"

"By all means." He noted that she was fixing his coffee just as he liked it, after having seen him drink coffee only once.

"Did you cancel my wake-up call?"

Travis accepted the cup she held out. "Guilty. I thought you could probably use the sleep."

"Thoughtful of you. Is that your game plan, by the way?"

Picking up his fork, he looked at her, then smiled. "You're a suspicious wench."

"You'll have to forgive me. It's just that I've learned one of life's ironclad rules."

"Which is?"

"People who claim they're after nothing are always after something."

Serious now, Travis studied her as she apparently concentrated on her meal. "And so you think I'm after more than your company?"

"It crossed my mind."

"Such as?"

"I haven't figured that out yet."

"The truth about your past, perhaps?" he offered slyly.

"I *know* you're after that. And something else as well."

"You're a very perceptive lady."

"Thank you." She looked at him. "What are you after, Travis?"

"Would you believe me if I said I was chasing a dream?"

Something flickered briefly in her eyes, then died. "No."

"Cynical," he mocked softly.

"I don't make pretty speeches," she said. "I don't like hearing them."

"Yes," he said thoughtfully. "I imagine you've been flattered quite a lot in your life, haven't you?" When she said nothing, but only continued to gaze at him steadily, Travis sighed. "And you don't take any bait dangled in front of you, do you?"

She answered that, a twinkle in her eyes. "No, I don't. I've done a bit of fishing, Travis, and I'm well aware that bait always contains a hook. So why don't you just reel your line in?"

"I will . . . if you'll drop your guard."

Saber tossed her napkin aside and sat back, studying him intently. "You'd like that, wouldn't you?"

"Yes, I would," he replied. "Because as enjoyable as it is to fence with you, Saber, the mental exercise isn't bringing me a bit closer to the woman I want to know. No pretty speeches. No Spanish coin. I want to get to know you very badly, and this past of yours—which we've both made too damn much of—is standing in my way."

"So if I drop my guard," she murmured, "you'll leave my past where it belongs—in the past?"

He nodded. "For the time being, at least. I'm being honest. There may well come a time when I'll need to know who you were yesterday; right now, I want to know who you are today."

"Revising our bargain somewhat?"

"No. The bargain was that I'd agree not to write about you if you agreed to treat me simply as a man who's attracted to you. That hasn't changed."

After a moment, Saber spoke very slowly. "During the past few months, I've held to a grueling schedule in the recording studio and on the road. I planned a month's vacation in a quiet place, where I intend to relax and forget schedules." She took a deep breath. "I don't want to have to be on guard for two weeks out of that month. I don't want to be afraid that every innocent word I say will be probed and examined as a possible clue to my past. If I find that happening, Travis, then I'll consider that I've fulfilled my end of the bargain— and that'll be the end of it."

"Agreed," he said promptly. "All I ask is that you make allowances for a naturally...inquisitive nature." He grinned. "I may well ask questions about Saber Duncan, but I'll do my best to forget she was ever anyone else."

THREE

SABER GAZED AT him for a moment, weighing, measuring. For an instant, she was tempted to end it here and now. A single phone call would put an army at her back, a quietly efficient army that would move Travis out of her life with no fuss or bother to herself.

To a man of Travis's intelligence, however, that action would be not only a stimulus to search out her past, but also a clue to finding that past.

Saber dared not take that chance.

Slowly she nodded, accepting his word and accepting the responsibility of protecting herself on her own. Protecting herself . . .

"You look so lost," he said quietly. "Why?"

Saber's throat tightened as she stared at him, and she fought a second impulse to end it now. She was vulnerable, tired and vulnerable, and he was too dangerously perceptive a man to gamble her life on. "You're seeing things," she said, resisting the impulse again.

"You were going to drop your guard," he reminded her, still quiet.

Looking into the depths of his serious green eyes, Saber felt the same sensation as last night. The room was shrinking, he was filling it with his presence, and she heard herself respond to his eyes rather than his voice. "When you guard . . . anything . . . long enough, it isn't easy to stop."

After a moment, he tossed his napkin aside and rose. Stepping around the table, he bent to grasp her hands and pulled her to her feet. Softly, he said, "You're a beautiful woman, Saber. A woman who can haunt a man's dreams even wearing a flannel nightgown. A woman who makes a man remember he *is* a man. Can't we forget everything else for now?"

Saber tried to collect her thoughts, but it was impossible: she was too conscious of the warm hands holding hers. No man had ever come so close, said such words, gazed at her with such intensity. She was torn, a lifelong wariness leaving her feeling threatened and a newfound awareness stirring excitement somewhere within her.

"I don't know," she said at last. "Can we?"

Travis gazed down at her, a muscle tightening in his jaw. He knew that he, at least, could forget everything but what she was in this moment—a woman he wanted until his body ached with desire.

Huskily, he said, "I want you. I know that." Before she could make more than an instinctive attempt to pull away from him, Travis released her hands only to draw her suddenly, powerfully, against the hard length of his body. "I'll make you forget everything else," he breathed, and then his mouth found hers.

Saber had believed until then that she knew what desire felt like, but the distant memory of a man's arms around a girl faded to nothing as Travis held her. Panicked, she tried to douse the flames rising inside of her, fighting to keep something as wild as unreason caged deep within her. It was as if she were onstage, a part of her seeking an outlet in the faceless audience. But Travis was not faceless or nameless ... or safe.

She could feel the strength of his body against hers, feel his heart pounding beneath her hand. And the lips slanting hungrily across hers drew desire from an unsuspected well at the core of her being. Who she was, what she was, what she had been—none of it mattered. In that moment, nothing mattered but the flames she felt licking at the bars of a cage.

Of their own volition, her hands slid up his chest until her fingers could tangle in the silky darkness of his hair. She wanted to be close to him, closer; she needed the strength of him. Caution withered in the heat blazing almost out of control.

Saber drew a ragged breath as his lips left hers,

her eyes opening slowly, heavily. She stared up into green eyes gone impossibly dark, and an old instinct told her then that Travis threatened her future with more than knowledge of her past. He threatened her future with himself. If this stranger could make her feel this way . . .

As if he saw or sensed the beginnings of withdrawal, Travis kissed her again, fierce but oddly teasing as well. And with his kiss, the passion that had flickered uncertainly, then died to embers, now blazed anew.

It was curiously more compelling than outright hunger, bringing her senses alive in a surging rush of feelings. A heated tingle swirled to life somewhere inside her and spread outward in ripples of sensation.

A kiss, she thought dimly, astonished. Just a kiss!

When Travis lifted his head again, his breathing was rough and uneven, the darkened eyes hot. "That's what we have, what we are," he said hoarsely. "It's all that matters right now, Saber. We can forget the rest."

Stunned by her own response, Saber allowed her arms to fall away, backing a step as he released her. She wanted to tell him to leave, to get out of her life, but something stopped the words—something she couldn't fight. And that frightened her because she had learned to fight elements stronger than any man could ever be.

"We can forget the rest," he repeated, steadier now.

Saber stared at him, uncertain. But when his eyes flickered downward to focus briefly on her mouth, she felt an instant surge of longing. "For now," she murmured. "We can forget...for now."

Travis drew a deep breath and released it slowly. "That's all I'm asking, Saber. For now, we'll forget everything except that we're a man and woman with something between us." Determined to hear her admit it, he added. "You can't deny that."

It wasn't a question: Saber knew it was a demand. And his eyes drew the truth from her before she could even consider evasion. "I can't deny that."

Travis smiled at her, his eyes still darkened and warm. "Where do we go from here?"

She decided to take the question literally and was just about to tell him where her vacation retreat was when the phone rang. With a slight gesture, she went to answer it, a bit startled to find the caller was her manager.

"Hello, Phil. What's up?"

Travis only half listened to her end of the conversation at first, too occupied with watching her lovely face in profile and trying to calm his still racing pulse. Not that he could do that while his eyes rested on her and his thoughts were filled with her. Then she half turned to glance at him, and something in the depths of her silvery eyes drew his attention to the conversation.

"No, no, you were right to let me know. Yes, but the exposure's worth it. What about the band?" She glanced at her watch. "They should be arriving in L.A. about now. Oh, have you? No, I don't think we'll need that. Tell them to take it easy until late tomorrow afternoon; we'll run through it once, but I don't think we need more than that.

Right. Oh—and Phil?" Her eyes lifted to Travis again fleetingly. "Book two rooms for me, will you? Two separate rooms. No questions. All right. I will. Bye, Phil." Saber cradled the receiver slowly.

"What was that all about?" Travis asked.

Saber sat down at the end of the couch and looked at him thoughtfully. "We've been trying to get a booking in Kansas City for the past year, but all schedules were filled. They've had a cancellation for tomorrow night. Phil's already put the band on a plane out there: he knew I'd want it. They'll advertise heavily on radio and television to alert the public."

"Another concert?"

"That's right."

Travis was conscious of a curious feeling then. Not jealousy, but an inexplicable conviction that she would slip away from him once she stepped onstage again. She was guarded and elusive once more, the brief conversation with her manager having partially erected the walls he had fought his way through only moments before: she was hiding again behind a serene veil.

Bothered by that and by the weariness he had glimpsed in her eyes, Travis focused on the concrete. "Saber, you've done twelve cities in twelve days already. You need to rest."

"I'll fly out this afternoon and rest tonight," she said. "A short rehearsal tomorrow afternoon, then the performance."

Whether she intended it or not, Travis caught the subtle intimation in her words. *She* would fly out today: she could admit to there being something between them, but she would link them together in no other way. He sighed roughly. "I see. Is the extra room for me?"

"I'd hate for you to have to sleep on a couch again. If you're coming, that is."

"We've settled that." He was abrupt and tried to dampen the frustration he felt.

"All right, then," she said softly.

"Saber . . ."

"What?"

"Don't look at me like I'm a stranger."

She quickly looked away, almost hating him because he kept slipping through her guard. "You are a stranger. Look, why don't we go ahead and get an early start to Kansas City? We can—" She rose as she spoke, breaking off abruptly when he crossed to stand before her and grasp her hands firmly. He said nothing for a moment, just lifted their hands until she could see them. And she saw before she felt: her fingers had twined instantly with his of their own volition. Slowly, she met his steady gaze.

"You're so damned elusive," he said in a soft, raspy tone of voice. His fingers tightened on hers. "But you don't want to be, Saber. The way you respond to my touch tells me that."

She stared at him mutely, unable to deny or defend. She was tired and she knew it. Too tired to do a show in Kansas City. Too tired to cope with bewildering new feelings and unnerving fears. And Travis must have realized because the expression on his face softened.

"All right," he said on a sigh, squeezing her hands gently before releasing them. "I'll try to back off a little. But it won't be easy." His gaze dropped to glide down over her body. "It won't be easy at all."

Saber took a step back, startled because when his eyes had touched her it was as if his hands had. She turned away, hoping to hide the reaction, speaking automatically. "Why don't we get started?"

Thinking back on it, she decided later that that had been a loaded question.

They talked little until the Lear had left Chicago far behind, and even then the silences were long between them. Saber, always tensely occupied with controlling her fear before flying, found on this trip that awareness of a man could push even this strong a fear aside. She was almost painfully conscious of him sitting by her side, aware of words and silences and the woodsy scent of his cologne.

She had fought hard to gain control of her life, and what was happening to her now, she knew, was beyond her ability to control. The caged part of her surged and throbbed toward an outlet, toward freedom, and only the stage offered that. Until now. Now that restless force within her had been stirred to life by Travis, and it leaned toward him like a flower to the sun.

Saber wished the performance were only scant hours away, wished she could step out onto a stage instantly and free the wildness before it overwhelmed her. Before that part of her broke free of its own strength and reached for the outlet Travis offered.

She pushed that thought away violently even as steady hands landed the jet with automatic awareness. But she wanted to find a corner somewhere and creep into it, hide, until she understood what was happening to her.

By the time they reached their hotel and checked in, she had found that corner. In a sense. She had always faced her fears, but what she felt now was too nebulous to confront; so Saber turned away from it, ignored it. She clung to the one reality she knew to be certain—that of living from heartbeat to heartbeat. And if each beat throbbed a man's name, she was unwilling to face that now.

Phil had reserved separate rooms all right. A two-bedroom suite. A large and expensive suite that was very beautiful and very private. Saber avoided the look she felt directed at her from Travis, hoping vaguely that no gossip-hungry reporter found out. And, she reminded herself, it was only for two nights. What could happen in two nights?

"You should rest," Travis said when the bell-man had gone.

Saber moved restlessly to turn a blind gaze to the view outside their sitting room window, knowing from experience that rest wouldn't help her. Only an explosive performance would drain her to the point of not thinking and hardly feeling— which was what she wanted, needed.

"I'm not tired," she said, and it was only partly a lie. She wasn't tired enough. Unconsciously, she tried to ease tense shoulders, stiffening even more when she felt his presence behind her and his hands move to gently probe taut muscles.

"You're tense," he said quietly.

She closed her eyes, his touch half pain and half pleasure. "It's just...preperformance jitters."

His long fingers continued to knead firmly and gently, soothing even as she was made more stingingly aware of him. She could feel the heat of him through her sweater and fought the urge to lean back against him. One of his hands slid down to probe the small of her back, stroking in a tiny, gentle circle until she felt weakness invade her knees. She wanted to tell him to stop, but when his other hand slipped beneath her hair to rub the nape of her neck, she could only let her head fall forward in mute acceptance.

There had been little touching in her life, and she realized only dimly that a part of her was hungry for touch. His touch. Wary of that, she forced her body to shift away from him. But the hand at her back moved around to encircle her waist, holding her in place.

"Travis—"

"You're such a tiny thing." His voice was soft, his tone whimsical. His hand lay over her flat stomach, fingers spread, the thumb just beneath the swell of her breasts. "Onstage you explode like a tiny dynamo, sending current in a dozen directions at once. And offstage...offstage you hold that inside as if it's a life force you're afraid to waste. Where's the switch, Saber? What turns that current on? Is it the singing itself? Or do you reflect the power an audience feeds you? Is it yours...or is it theirs?"

Saber bit her lip against the cry, *Mine! I earned it!* He wouldn't understand, and she would not fling what she was at the feet of a stranger. But he didn't seem to expect an answer.

"When I touch you," he murmured, "I can almost feel that power. Like fire surging just beneath the skin. It's addictive, Saber. I have to touch you."

"What do you want from me?" she cried suddenly, breaking away and whirling to stare at him. Intense green eyes met hers.

"That," he breathed. "The part you only give an audience. That's what I want."

Saber shook her head. "You don't know what you're talking about," she said huskily.

"Do you?"

It was an odd question, and she stared at him in bewilderment.

Travis reached out to touch her cheek, his fingers lingering. As if to himself, he murmured, "No, you have to be aware of it. You have to know it's more than stage presence."

Trying to defend that hidden part of her, Saber unwillingly faced what she wanted to avoid. "You said we'd forget everything except what's between us," she reminded him.

"But that's it, Saber," he told her, intensity creeping into his voice. "That is what's between us. Don't you see? That's why I have to touch you, and why you have to respond."

She took a step back, feeling cornered, both excitement and fear flickering inside her. For a moment, she wondered if he did somehow spark that caged part of her. Then she denied the possibility with inner violence. If he was right, it would change her life forever. If he was wrong...if he was wrong...

"I'm going to take a shower," she said with forced calm. "Do whatever you like about dinner; I'm going to order room service."

"I'll order for both of us," he said. "No need for them to make two trips."

Saber headed for her bedroom and closed the door behind her, shutting out him and his last quiet words.

"Elusive. Always just out of reach."

She changed her mind and took a long bath instead of a shower, hoping an immersion in hot water would draw the tension from her body. But the tension remained; what seeped away, she realized later, was a large chunk of her stubborn willpower.

Wary of spending too much time alone with Travis, Saber didn't return to the sitting room after her bath. Only half-aware of her actions—and motivations—she chose the most shapeless nightgown in her case, not a flannel affair but one made of thick terry cloth that reached to the floor. Then she stretched out on the wide bed and closed her eyes.

Saber was not given to afternoon naps; the driving energy that had taken her to the top of her profession in a short year tended to fill her days with action, with movement. But sleep was nature's restorative, and both Saber's anxious mind and tense body demanded it.

She woke to the vague realization of hours having passed unnoticed, conscious of the lazy heaviness of her still body. Conscious of that and of the quiet green eyes watching her.

"I didn't pour water on you," he said, his voice curiously soft, his smile crooked. "Even though our dinner will be here in a few minutes."

Drowsy, Saber looked at him. Her sleep-fogged mind could identify no threat here, no reason to be guarded or wary. And her body, still gripped by the inertia of sleep, resisted even awareness. "Thank you," she murmured.

"You're welcome." His hand moved to lay gently over hers where it rested, motionless, on the bedspread. Then his fingers curled around hers and her hand was lifted to touch his lips.

Saber watched the movement, a part of her mind idly considering his gentleness. She felt the warmth of his hand and lips, but it was a sensation hovering on the edge of her perceptions and failed to alarm her.

Watching her, Travis wanted to hold his breath for fear she would realize what she was at this moment and hide from him again. Still at the edge of sleep, she was vulnerable; she was a lovely, delicate girl with a sweet face and gentle gray eyes, and he had only seen her before in a two-year-old photo. She looked at him curious and wondering, as a girl would look upon a man she might see before her as she rounded a corner. No alarm shadowed her eyes.

The controlled woman he'd known until now fascinated him, the flickering wildness in her eyes sparking something deep within him; her every movement drew his gaze, the feline beauty of her nearly stopped his heart. But this girl, so still and quiet, her dreamy eyes pondering some mystery, this girl did stop his heart. He wanted to reach out and hold her, protect her against what the world would do to her. He wanted to wrap her in his arms to shut out cold reality. He wanted to build a world for her.

But Travis dared make no sudden move and dared not question, even silently, what he felt. Carefully, he sought to hold the moment.

"Who are you?" she asked suddenly, and it didn't seem an odd question.

"Who am I?" His voice was husky, low. "I'm a man who loves children and animals and spring showers. I play tennis and swim and ride horses. I read books because ideas fascinate me, and I listen to music because my soul needs to hear it. That's who I am, Saber."

Still dreamy, she gazed at him. "Why are you here?"

Even more softly, he said, "Because I saw a shooting star one night and heard a voice I couldn't believe."

"Will you catch the star?" she asked.

"Only if you let me," he whispered, and bent

forward, still holding her hand, to kiss her tenderly.

Saber felt the soft warmth of his lips, the feathery touch that was gentle and undemanding, and something deep inside of her uncurled tentatively to bask in that glowing feeling. She touched his cheek with her free hand as he slowly drew away, a gesture without thought or will but prompted by a need beyond reason.

Not even harsh knocks on the sitting room door had the power to disturb her.

"Dinner," he murmured, looking down at her with a peculiarly intense light in his green eyes.

She nodded, feeling bereft when he released her hand and rose to his feet. She watched him leave her bedroom to deal with the waiter, then sat up and slid from the bed reluctantly. The last tendrils of sleep were leaving her, but she held on to this odd, softened mood; she could remember feeling like this, but the memory was a distant one. Not the distance of time, but the distance of experience.

Saber stood just inside the sitting room, staring at his broad shoulders as he closed the door behind the waiter. She was conscious of something fragile being in the room with them, something a careless word or gesture could destroy in an instant. Uneasiness flickered within her, a dim realization of her own vulnerability, but she dismissed it as he turned to face her.

The softened, fragile mood held—for a while. They ate their meal, watching as the night aged outside their windows, speaking quietly about inconsequential things. Travis watched her unobtrusively, still feeling as if he held his breath. The banked desires within him stirred, but he kept them under control, driven even more strongly by an urge to understand this gentle side of her.

Then, when the dinner remains had been sent away, they were left, alone with nothing to occupy them. Nothing but each other and a growing awareness.

Saber tried to ignore the restlessness, needing the brief peace she had felt. But there was something inside of her stronger than peace, something that had napped longer than her body and was now awakening within her. She wanted to cry out in protest as she found herself pacing, found herself keeping distance between herself and Travis.

He was dangerous. That was what she had to remember. Against her will, she remembered a gentle kiss and an odd, hot tenderness in green eyes, and her thoughts shied violently.

"Saber?"

His deep voice seemed to play over her taut nerves like a physical caress, and when she turned from the window to face him it was with the stiff, jerky motion of reluctance.

Travis rose from the chair where he had watched her pacing, feeling his own face tighten as he saw the wariness in hers. Regret flowed through him, regret and frustration and a growing bewilderment. "How many women are you, Saber?" he mused. "What in your life divided you like this?"

"We were going to leave my past out of this," she reminded him, holding herself still when she wanted so badly to— What? She didn't know. Except that she *wanted*.

He stepped toward her, the movement putting

his face in shadow as the lamp behind him silhouetted his lean body. "I don't care who you were," he said, his voice strained. "Not now. I only care about who you are. But you won't let me get close. You won't let me *in*."

Saber took a deep breath, fighting the temptation to tell him anything he wanted to know. Dimly, she realized that what had once seemed a wonderful and exciting secret to a child had become a woman's intolerable burden. She wondered when that had happened; had it been instantaneous or a gradual thing? Had she awakened one morning to the shocked realization of what she was, what she would always be? Or had it come to her slowly over the years? When had her sense of power become a trap?

Dear God...she was so tired of hiding. And her escape from hiding had become a prison she had never intended. *This* was her prison. The prison of having no name, no past. The prison of gazing into a man's puzzled eyes and being unable to answer his questions.

Travis took another step toward her, his hand

lifting as though he would have touched her. But Saber turned quickly toward her bedroom, her tension so great, so brittle, that she guarded herself from his touch as she would have guarded fragile crystal from a blow.

She'd shatter. If he touched her, she would shatter, and the dear Lord only knew if she could put herself back together again.

"Good night, Travis," she said huskily.

He drew a deep breath, his hand falling. "Good night, Saber."

It was a long time before Travis went into his own bedroom. He stood at the window and gazed out into the night, the ache within him now a familiar pain.

FOUR

TRAVIS STOOD IN the wings, his gaze following Saber. The powerful lights turned her sequined evening gown to liquid gold, and her sensuous movements intensified that image. Music filled the huge building, and the roar from the audience was a steadily building force that seemed a living thing.

She was giving them everything inside her.

He felt it as he had before, as the audience felt it. He felt waves of power and passion emanating from the spotlighted woman until his throat tightened with emotion and his hands gripped her wrap convulsively.

It was difficult to think clearly, but Travis forced himself to remember this long day. She had been more than elusive, more than just out of reach. She had been gone. Only a note had greeted him this morning, a brief apology that she had "things to take care of." He had come here and waited, watching the band assemble, watching the rehearsal that had been explosive itself. Then she had disappeared again, leaving her gown here and having no reason to return to the hotel until after the performance.

It had been a very long day.

Travis, with little to do but think, came to several conclusions. In spite of the ache that left him sleepless, restless, he realized he could get no relief. If he pushed Saber too hard or too fast, she would put herself forever out of his reach. He realized that she would be even more wary because he had seen the vulnerable side of her. And he realized that—somehow—he had to convince her he was no threat.

He didn't know if he had the patience. His deepest instincts urged him to hold her tightly with the first firm grasp he could manage, but his mind warned him that he would never hold her unless she allowed him to. That would take time. And trust. If it came at all.

And now...

Travis listened to that naked voice, everything stripped from it but raw emotion. He watched her fling that powerful, invisible part of herself out into a faceless audience with the savage release of an electric current gone wild, and it crackled around her.

He had never seen her give so much, and when she stumbled from the stage he was quickly and silently there to drop the wrap around her shoulders and lead her toward the exit. They were too quick for the fans surging around the building to get a closer look at Saber; the limo pulled away even as the first shouts reached them.

She was tense beside him in the darkness, and Travis said nothing. He remained silent during the ride to the hotel and in the elevator up to their suite. His first words came only when she returned to the sitting room after showering and changing into a loose robe to find the coffee he had ordered waiting for her.

"I still don't agree with coffee this late," he said dryly, handing her a cup.

"It works for me." Saber sat down at the end of the long couch, her face nearly translucent with exhaustion.

He sat down near her, watching her sip the coffee. "You'll burn yourself out if you keep this up."

Saber smiled a little. "No. I can rest now." Then she sent him an oblique glance. "Or can I?"

Travis linked his fingers together and gazed down at them for a long moment. When his eyes lifted, something regretful and pained shimmered there. "I pushed," he said.

She knew he was referring to the day before, which had been answered by her disappearing act today. "You pushed." She nodded. "I don't like running away, Travis. Don't make me run away again."

"All right," he said quietly. "We'll just get to

know each other. You need rest after tonight...
after this tour...and we'll take all the time you
need for that. I promise, Saber."

"I'll hold you to that," she managed to say. The
glaze of her weariness was between them, and
Saber welcomed it. She didn't want to think about
anything for a while. Not what she was beginning
to feel for him. Not her past or future. Nothing. At
least for a while.

"Go to bed," he ordered gently.

She didn't think about arguing, either. She went
to bed.

Only the ringing of the phone disturbed their
breakfast the next morning. Saber had awakened
cheerful, her manner toward Travis light; clearly,
she was at least willing to accept his word for the
moment. And he was determined to make no more
mistakes. Patience had become his watchword.

With a faintly apologetic gesture, she rose and
went to sit on the couch, lifting the receiver from
its place on the end table. "Hello?"

Travis watched her unobtrusively as he finished his meal. He saw her face change, soften, even as it turned curiously wary.

"No, it went well," she said into the phone. "Yes, I am, and I'm planning to take a rest. Cory's place; it isn't crowded this time of the year, and I've taken a cottage. . . . The landing strip in Prescott, then a car." She frowned suddenly. "No, don't do that. I know what I—It's the back of beyond out there. There's no need to—" She listened to her caller in frowning silence for a moment, then spoke wryly. "I know there's a pad, but I'd really prefer not to make use of it. . . . *I'm* being unreasonable? Look, I'll arrange it, all right? Yes, I promise. Right. Bye."

Saber cradled the receiver and sat frowning at Travis for a moment.

"Is it something I've done?" he asked politely.

She blinked, then smiled. "No. Do you object to helicopters?"

"On principle, no," he answered, taking the question at face value.

"Good." She picked up the receiver again and

placed a long-distance call, reaching her party almost instantly. "Cory Stewart, please. Oh, hi. . . . No, but you sounded harassed. . . . Really? Well, everybody's curious about you and you can't blame them. . . . All right, since I value my neck, I'll shut up about that." She smiled a little, apparently listening to a somewhat lengthy response. "All right. Yes, I'll be heading your way in an hour or so. Cory, does Lee still fly his charter service? Oh, damn, I wanted to—You did? Well, I wondered when you'd get around to it. Can I trust you with my precious skin?" Her smile widened. "Don't be rude to a paying customer. Okay, I'll call you in about an hour and let you know when we'll be arriving. . . . Just a stray I picked up: can you spare him a room?" Saber grinned as Travis made a face at her, then briskly ended her conversation. "Great. I'll call in about an hour."

"Am I the stray you picked up?" Travis demanded as soon as she'd hung up.

"Just a figure of speech, Travis."

"Uh-huh." He stared at her. "Not that I mean to

pry, but who is Cory Stewart, and just where are we going?"

Saber returned to the table, sitting down and reaching for her coffee. "Cory Stewart is a friend of mine; she owns the place where we're going on *my* vacation. And we're going to Arizona."

"Arizona? What's in Arizona?"

She smiled at him gently. "A dude ranch."

Travis realized that his mouth was open and hastily closed it. "A dude ranch. I see."

He was still a bit bemused when the Lear taxied to a stop at a landing strip in Prescott, Arizona, some considerable time later—and not only because their destination was a dude ranch. Having accepted his word that he wanted only to get to know her, Saber had completely relaxed in his company. During the trip he'd discovered she had a mischievous sense of humor and a hypnotically sweet smile that revealed an elusive dimple.

"You'll love Cory; everybody does," she said as they stood beside the jet with their baggage. She had no time to say more but gestured slightly at the woman approaching them.

Travis blinked at the sight; he couldn't help it. From the few things Saber had mentioned about their hostess during the trip out here, he had evolved a mental image quite different from the reality. He'd imagined a brisk and cheerful woman, yes, but smaller. Considerably smaller.

Cory Stewart was dressed in jeans, a blue denim shirt, and running shoes rather than western boots, and she sported a billed cap atop a riotous mass of flaming red hair. Green-eyed and with a husky voice, she was a stunning woman somewhere in her midtwenties. And she was every inch of six feet tall.

It was obvious that the two women were good friends, and Cory looked Travis over with a critical but curiously indulgent eye as she shook hands with him briskly.

"So you're the stray, huh? Only Saber could call you that. I've read your books; you're good." Giving Travis no time at all to respond to her remarks, she directed the next few to Saber. "Jed'll guard your Lear with his life; he's even promised to wash it. C'mon—the chopper's this way." Then she grabbed a bag in either hand and strode off across the field.

"She's something, isn't she?" Saber murmured, picking up a small bag.

Travis took it away from her. "Does she command armies in her spare time?" he asked wryly.

As they trailed after their hostess, Saber replied, "The staff at the ranch would say so. For myself, I think she should work her talents on the United Nations. The world would be dazed—but better off."

He laughed, then meekly climbed aboard the blue-and-white helicopter when ordered to do so. Earphones made conversation possible within the craft when they'd lifted off, but Travis was a bit too unnerved by Cory's seat-of-the-pants flying techniques to contribute anything to the casual dialogue carried on by the women.

He wondered briefly why Saber's avowed fear of flying apparently didn't extend to this helicopter ride, then he filed the question away and concentrated instead on watching the dizzily passing scenery of mountains and valleys. Major highways appeared few and far between, and he realized that Saber's description of "the back of beyond" had been apt.

The phrase reminded him of her call and of the unidentified person she had talked to. Travis had ventured a single question during the trip from Kansas City, to which she'd replied simply, "No, I'd rather not tell you. Sorry." He had left it at that, but to say that he was curious would have been an understatement. It was yet another item he filed away for the future...the near future.

So wrapped up was he in his own brooding thoughts that Travis realized only belatedly that they'd arrived at their destination. Before he could get more than a glimpse of a sprawling expanse of buildings nestled in a beautiful valley, the helicopter dipped below tree level and settled itself with barely a thump on a concrete pad.

Cory talked to them vivaciously as they made their way along a graveled walkway toward the central building. It was a large three-story house with a wide porch on two sides, whitewashed and lovely. To the left, a four-rail fence framed a view of rolling pastureland, and to the right were other graveled paths leading to smaller buildings— cottages, Travis assumed. He could also see a couple of tennis courts, and a faint, distant splash hinted at the existence of a pool.

It didn't really look like the tourist conception of Arizona, but since he'd been in this part of the state before, Travis was not surprised.

"Saber can show you around," Cory told him in her innately warm and friendly voice. "She knows the place almost as well as I do. There are trails all through the mountains for walking or riding, a pool, and tennis courts. You can have your meals in the main house, have 'em sent to your cottage, or else ask to have your kitchen in the cottage stocked and do for yourself. We're pretty informal here; if we're having a party or special dinner, I ask that you wear shoes—otherwise you dress however you feel."

Travis laughed as they halted a few steps from the main house, then realized that Cory was eyeing them both rather sheepishly.

"There's just one—small—matter I'd better discuss with you."

"Cory, what've you done?" Saber demanded, instantly suspicious.

The glowing redhead pulled on an innocent expression. "I swear it wasn't intentional, Saber. How could it be? I didn't know you were bringing company until today."

"Out with it," Saber ordered.

"Well, we're not crowded this time of year, but the main house is full. I'd reserved a cottage for you, of course, but the others are being redecorated. The furniture's all shoved together under covers and there are paint buckets and the like. Well, anyway, the point is that you two are going to have to share a cottage."

Saber stared at her.

"It's a two bedroom," Cory offered, ridiculously hopeful.

Travis could have kissed her, but he maintained an expressionless face and waited for Saber to speak.

"What about my good name, friend?" She didn't look at Travis.

"You're a superstar—who expects you to have a good name?"

"Cory."

The redhead laughed. "Everybody minds their own business here, Saber, and you know it; that's why you come here. There isn't a journalist, gossip columnist, or any other kind of troublemaker within thirty miles of here. No fuss and no bother. Now, shall I make up a bed for Travis on the living room couch in the main house—where he'll quite likely be sat on—or are you going to share your cottage with him?"

Sighing, and with a feeling of trying to close the barn door after the livestock had escaped *anyway*. Saber gave in. "All right. Anything to keep you from telling everyone I'm a monster. And you would. I know you."

"I should hope so after ten years," Cory answered cheerfully.

At that moment, a harassed-looking young man appeared on the porch. "Cory, I need you!" he wailed, the fingers of both hands clutching his blond hair in a manner that appeared desperate rather than dramatic.

Cory dropped the single bag she'd managed to wrest away from Travis at the helicopter, saying obscurely, "Damn the woman. She's meddled with his paints again. It's number four, Saber." And as she dashed up the steps, she tossed over her shoulder at Travis, "D'you mind? I have to—" Then she'd taken the young man by the arm and steered him firmly into the house.

Travis only realized he was standing there with his mouth open when he heard Saber laughing. Closing his mouth, he stared down at her. "Mind telling me what that was all about?" he requested.

Saber bent to pick up the abandoned bag since Travis had his hands full with the other two. "The plea for help came from Mark," she explained, beginning to lead the way along one of the graveled paths. "He's sort of . . . a project of Cory's. He stays here several times a year and paints. As an artist, he's quite talented, but at day-to-day living, he's utterly hopeless. He has no temper whatsoever and depends on Cory to keep his world on an even keel, which she does."

"And what woman did Cory damn for meddling with the paints?"

"Jenny, the housekeeper. She's a jewel of a housekeeper, which, I suppose, is why she hates the smell of oil paint; she's always putting Mark's paints away neatly where he can't find them. Hence his very real panic."

Bemused, Travis shook his head. "Are the other . . . guests as strange as the artist?"

Saber turned off the main path onto a more narrow one leading through the trees. "Didn't you notice the plaque hanging at the main house?"

Travis vaguely recalled seeing a discreet sign but couldn't remember what had been written on it. "Yes, but not what it said."

"The Hideaway." Saber smiled up at him as they reached a small but lovely house tucked away in the woods. "This place was built twenty years ago by Cory's father. People come here for rest and peace. Average people, of course, but also very important people." She opened the door and led the way into a spacious, comfortably furnished living room.

Setting the bags down by the long couch, Travis looked around approvingly. But his mind returned to Saber's comments. "So you were pulling my leg by calling this place a dude ranch," he said.

"Something like that. Any preference as to bedrooms?" She had looked in both the rooms by then.

"No. You're taking these unforeseen arrangements very calmly, I must say."

She turned to show him a solemn face. "The bedroom doors have locks; I checked."

He realized then that his voice had been mildly aggrieved, and he had to laugh. "All right, so you've surprised me. In fact, you keep surprising me. In thirty-two years, I've never encountered anyone like you."

Smiling, she picked up her bags. "I'll take this bedroom," she said, choosing the one to the right of the living room.

Travis carried his bag to the bedroom on the

left, and they unpacked in a companionable silence broken only by occasional comments.

"You didn't come prepared for this trip like I did," she called to him at one point. "You went to the city to meet a singer and ended up crossing the country to a ranch. If you need anything in the way of clothing, there's a store on the grounds that sells everything. And the laundry service here is as good as anyone could want."

"I'll have to take advantage of both services," he called back. Finishing his own unpacking first, he went out into the living room and from there to the adjoining kitchen. He explored thoroughly, finding the cabinets stocked with snacks and the refrigerator with soft drinks and various fruit juices. When Saber came out of her bedroom, he was seated comfortably on the couch with a glass of orange juice in his hand and a second glass on the coffee table.

She picked up the second glass and sat in an overstuffed chair across from him, smiling. "Won't anyone be concerned about you? Dropping out of sight so suddenly, I mean?" she asked.

Travis shook his head. "Nope. I travel fairly often and never keep to a firm schedule. The book I'd planned to do on you was an idea I'd kept to myself, so my publisher isn't expecting to hear from me."

"No lady friend to be alarmed by your absence?" Her voice was light.

With another slight shake of his head, Travis replied, "No."

Peculiarly conscious of his steady gaze, Saber rose hastily. "Come on—I'll show you around the place."

Having admitted to exhaustion after following Saber through only four cities of her tour, Travis requested that they spend a couple of days just resting without taking advantage of some of the more strenuous activities offered by The Hideaway. Saber had a sneaking suspicion that he was more concerned with her exhaustion and his own promise, but she said nothing about it.

So their first few days were spent quietly together. Neither had placed an undue emphasis on sharing the cottage—Travis because it suited him perfectly and Saber because of a loneliness she would never have admitted to him—and that unplanned intimacy put them rapidly on companionable terms. They took short, leisurely walks around the grounds, talked easily about likes and dislikes, and generally found they had enough in common to surprise them both. They argued mildly over Travis's fixed intention of paying for half the cost of "their" vacation, spent quiet evenings in the clubhouse listening to the small band, and developed a nodding acquaintance with most of the twenty-odd guests staying in the main house.

Between the warm, soporific, late summer days and the undemanding friendship, Saber all but forgot that Travis posed any threat to her peace. She had never before known the male companionship of a brother, friend, or lover and was surprised by how much she enjoyed his company. And it was a new experience for her to spend time with a man who wanted nothing from her—except the truth.

Whether his tactics were deliberate or not, Travis was following exactly the right path toward that truth. Saber, for the first time in a long while, was tempted to confide the past he was so interested in. She found it easy to talk to him, easy to laugh with him. A lifetime of guardedness was melting away.

Still, it was easy to be unguarded when there was no threat, easy to relax with no tension in the air. And inevitable that there would be a change.

If asked, Saber could have pointed to the moment when her own awareness roused her from the limbo of serene acceptance. Just as the veils had lifted briefly from her eyes in weariness late one night—and in the fleeting moments when a part of her had slept—so those veils were lifted again by a few chance words. Lifted for good.

They had taken a picnic lunch out into the rolling pasture, finding a peaceful, shady spot on the bank of a small stream. Horses grazed in the distance, incurious, and a faint breeze stirred the trees and the meadow grass. The scene perfectly suited the quiet mood of the past few days, and neither of them was in a hurry to pack up the remains of lunch.

Lazy conversation had died into a sweet silence as they sprawled on the blue-checked blanket borrowed from the cottage closet. The silence was shattered, however, when Mark appeared suddenly with a large sketchpad, a handful of charcoal pencils, and a hopeful look on his amiable face.

"Would you pose for me?" he asked, looking from one to the other with his shy smile.

"Do we have anything better to do?" Saber asked Travis.

"I'm game." Travis had been formally introduced to Mark the first day, although he couldn't help but realize that to the artist every human being but Cory was no more than a possible subject.

Laying his pad and pencils aside, Mark proved the force of this realization by briskly and critically arranging his subjects as if they were a still life of fruit or flowers on a table. He placed a meek Travis on his side and raised on one elbow with his other arm lying over an upraised knee, a wide tree trunk at his back. Saber was commanded to sit demurely at his waist and lean back, turning slightly so that her back rested against Travis's raised thigh and her left forearm lay across his ribs.

The position, both silently realized, was one that lovers might have assumed. They were left gazing at one another in an amused silence that insidiously became something else.

Mark, happily unaware of having disturbed his subjects, settled himself some little distance away with his sketchpad on his knees. "I've wanted you two for days," he murmured, turning to a blank sheet and setting to work. "The perfect couple. No, don't frown at me," he admonished Saber as she turned her head to stare at him. "It's lovely, but it isn't you. Look at Travis. Yes. Pensive. And he looks at you as he always does. Waiting. Yearning."

Saber gazed into green eyes that flickered briefly in surprise, then steadied to a faintly questioning look. She felt breathless beneath that look, and confused. Mark's comments unsettled her; was the artist simply creating a mood, or was he, as seemed obvious from his words, merely looking for expressions he'd seen on them both these past days? And if he had seen Travis gaze at her with yearning—why hadn't she seen that?

"Oh, damn—I've broken the point on the number three. I'll have to go and get another. Don't move," Mark ordered his subjects, then tenderly put aside his pad and hurried off toward the main house.

Saber took the opportunity to look anywhere but into those green eyes.

"It looks like our amiable artist has let the cat out of the bag," Travis said quietly.

"Really?" She forced a lightness into her voice.

"He caught me wearing my heart on my sleeve. I should have remembered how perceptive any good artist is."

She felt the warmth of his thigh through his jeans and her thin cotton blouse, and her fingers were suddenly far too aware of the lean ribs beneath his knit shirt. Green eyes drew her gaze, caught and held her captive. "He . . . must have been mistaken," she finally managed to say.

"No. He wasn't mistaken."

Saber would have drawn away at that, but the arm behind her abruptly encircled her shoulders and pulled her so close she could feel his warm breath on her face.

"You've treated me like a friend these past few days, Saber, and I'm glad you trust me enough for that," he said huskily. "Can you trust me enough to believe that I love you?"

Stunned, Saber couldn't think. And there was no resistance in her when his hand slipped to the nape of her neck and drew her head toward him until his lips found hers. Hungry, demanding, he kissed her as though afraid he would never get another chance, and Saber could no more stand against that than she could willingly stop breathing.

She was not a reckless or naive woman, but she forgot everything in that moment. It didn't seem to matter that they'd known each other for such a short time, or that he actually knew very little about her. The only thing that mattered was the warmth of his embrace, the compelling need of his kiss. Her body came to life in a way she'd never known before, vibrantly alive and aching with desire. Her hand lifted to touch his cheek, and Saber renounced the world.

But the world wouldn't go away.

"You moved," Mark said indignantly. "Yes, that's very pretty, but not what I had in mind!"

FIVE

SABER WAS FORCED to call on all her reserves of self-control to remain placid while Mark concluded their "sitting." Obeying the artist, she gazed into Travis's eyes, forcing her expression into the mold Mark requested. Pensive, he insisted.

Pensive? She thought about that, because it was slightly less unsettling than thinking of what the artist had seen in Travis's face. Pensive. Sad, wistfully reflective.

What had she to be sad about? As Travis had

said—she had fame, success, more money than she could ever spend. She had youth, health, friends. Why, then, had Mark seen sadness?

"Saber!"

Startled, she looked toward the young artist to find him frowning at her.

"You're moving," he complained.

Glancing down, Saber realized that the heel of her right hand was rubbing steadily, unconsciously, against her upper thigh. She halted the movement and turned her eyes back to Travis.

Softly, he said, "You do that often."

"What?" she murmured.

His green gaze flicked downward to a point half-way up from her knee, then lifted again to her face. "Rub your leg as if it aches. But you never seem to realize you're doing it."

It was another mental jolt, and one Saber could have done without. Though the gesture Travis and the artist had noticed was unconscious, she knew, of course, that it had become a habit. Now, she couldn't think of anything to say in response to Travis's comment.

Suddenly the artist closed his sketchbook and rose, a look of mild disgust in his amiable face. "It's no good," he told them. "I've lost you today. Maybe we can try again later?" He didn't wait for a response but immediately headed toward the main house.

Saber occupied herself with scrambling to her feet and gathering their picnic things together. She didn't look at Travis. So Mark had "lost them" for the moment? Travis's face had gone unreadable, she'd noted, and her own expression had most likely become unreadable, too, in an effort to guard against betraying her thoughts. She wondered vaguely if Mark would ever be able to capture expressions of which both she and Travis were now painfully aware.

And why had she gazed into Travis's eyes and felt—again—that she was seeing him for the first time? *Still waters run deep.* Now what, she wondered, did that cliché have to do with anything? It was just Mark making her aware, of course. Had to be.

"Saber?"

His quiet voice caught all her attention, but she still refused to look at him as she folded the blanket they'd so recently lain on. "Yes?"

"Don't let it spoil things."

She realized he was on his feet and standing close behind her. *Too close,* she thought, and experienced the unnerving certainty that it was not his physical nearness but something far more elusive that had panicked her. "I don't know what you mean," she said, again imposing an iron self-control.

He caught her shoulder suddenly, turning her to face him; she looked up instinctively—and wished she hadn't. There was an understanding on his face, in his green eyes, that she'd never seen before.

"You're like a touch-me-not flower," he said quietly. "Someone comes too near and you close up. What is it you're afraid to let anyone see, Saber? What are you hiding?"

She didn't say, "Nothing," because it would have been a lie. But Travis didn't seem to expect an answer.

He held her shoulders gently, ignoring the

folded blanket she clutched almost like a shield between them. "I don't want to rush you. I don't want you to feel I'm asking more than you can give. But I can't deny my own feelings, Saber."

"You don't know me." It was someone else's voice she heard, and it was gritty with emotions she wouldn't let herself understand.

"I know what I feel," he insisted firmly. Green eyes searched her face. "I love you, Saber."

She stepped back. "No."

"Saber—"

"D'you mind taking everything back to the cottage?" She tossed him the blanket. "I want . . . I need to be alone for a while."

Clearly reluctant, his expression anxious, Travis nonetheless nodded in acceptance. "All right. But Saber . . . don't go too far?"

She knew he wasn't referring to physical distance. Nodding, she headed off through the woods, making instinctively for a mountain path she knew well. It took an hour or more before she reached her favorite spot: a cluster of large boulders that jutted out from the mountainside, providing a breathtaking view of the valley below.

Saber climbed onto the largest of the boulders, allowing her legs to dangle over the edge. She had no fear of heights, and the dizzying drop from her seat to the valley floor earned no more than a careless glance from her. She looked out over the valley, absently watching the distant movements of Cory's guests.

The panic died away only gradually; she didn't try to think until even the faintest echoes of alarm had vanished. Then, very carefully, she etched an analysis in her mind.

Travis's avowed love frightened her. Why? Because she was afraid of love? No. Afraid of him? No. What was it he'd called her? A touch-me-not flower.

His understanding seemed to be—had to be—instinctive. He knew nothing of her past, nothing of the months "missing" from her life. Yet he saw a touch-me-not plant wincing away from contact. A flower that would open cheerfully to warmth and light but shrink from a touch. Not a physical touch, but the touch of someone . . . too close.

Was that she?

It was disturbing to think of herself in that way. She didn't *want* to be that way. Yet now that she considered it, she realized her entire life had molded just that trait. Guardedness, a sense of wariness where other people were concerned. Never allowing anyone to get too close, never letting her inner self be touched.

Until Travis.

Pushing all emotion aside with an effort, Saber made use of the "worst" scenario she had taught herself in order to keep things in perspective. What was the worst that could happen if she became more deeply involved with Travis? She could give her heart and be left empty and alone. Could she take the worst and refuse to let it destroy her? She didn't know.

A part of her wanted badly to reach for what Travis offered. He was an intelligent, humorous, sensitive man, possessing an innate warmth and a great sexuality that drew her strongly. Instinct told her now that he would keep her secrets as well as she could herself, but she had no idea how those secrets would affect their tenuous relationship.

It was ironic in a way. Always, she'd wanted to be loved for what she was, not who she was. She'd fought to escape a life thick with the risk of being taken at value of face—or bank account. Now, by her own ability, she was again a *who,* a personage. As he'd said . . . a larger-than-life personality.

Which did Travis believe he loved—that larger-than-life person or the woman he barely knew? Could it matter to him that that part of her had been born in a hell of survival?

He was fascinated by the abrupt change from girl to woman, and she couldn't help wondering if he, too, would prefer the girl she had been to the woman she now was.

Was that what she feared? That he would learn the truth of her physical and emotional catharsis and, the mystery solved, fold up his tent and steal away into her past? Case solved and on to elusive horizons? It was fun, sweetie, and let's do it again sometime?

Saber smiled in spite of herself. No, Travis would never be flippant. He thought that he loved her; she believed that. Only time could sort out her own tangled emotions, and only time and honesty could prove his to be real.

Thoughtfully, she climbed down off the boulder and began the walk back to the ranch. There was still a ghostly panic in the back of her mind; she expected it and accepted it with equanimity. She was strong enough, she believed, to be able to deal with that. And strong enough to take a chance, because she'd realized sometime during the past moments that she had to.

She was already half in love with Travis Foxx.

He was waiting for her near the valley floor, leaning on a whitewashed fence and watching as she approached. She could see as well as feel a certain tautness in him, a tense waiting, and felt a sudden compunction that she'd left him so abruptly. Something he needed to know about her. . . .

"I'm sorry, Travis," she said as she reached him.

"A habit of mine: whenever I'm bothered I go off alone to think things through. I should have explained."

He smiled, still watchful. "I'll remember next time."

They turned to follow the fence line back toward the still-distant cluster of buildings, and she felt a sudden warmth when he reached to clasp her hand firmly.

"And did you think things through?"

She nodded. "I tried."

"Will I be getting my marching orders?" he asked lightly.

But she could hear the strain. And it was an odd strain, she thought, confused. Again she had an instinctive urge to walk away and avoid...what? Something dangerous. Like a volcano churning at its core: unthreatening on the outside, but potentially overpowering.

Saber pushed the thoughts aside. "Not unless you want them."

"I don't." A roughness crept into his voice, but

he cleared his throat before continuing. "And so, Miss Duncan? We go on from here?"

Saber took a deep breath and nodded again. "I can't—promise anything, Travis. I don't know if I can give you what you want, and I don't know what I want myself. But I won't send you away. Or run away myself."

His fingers tightened slightly. "You're afraid, aren't you? But you're going to face it."

She no longer felt startled by his perception. "I don't like to allow fear to control me. I may... shy away from time to time. But I'll have to face it."

Travis was quiet for a while; they were almost at the main house before he spoke. "If I push, tell me."

"All right."

He stopped just as they approached the path to their cottage, gazing down at her with warm, restless eyes. "How can I help?"

Saber didn't have to think. "Make me laugh." She felt suddenly that she wanted to cry, and was surprised. She hadn't cried in a long time. In spite of the urge, she found herself smiling. "Teach me how to open up. Just be yourself, Travis."

Travis took her at her word. But he remained cautious, careful, unwilling to move too fast or step too near. She was a complex woman, much of her buried beneath the surface, and he'd known from the first that he would fully understand her only when she gave him her complete trust.

That the trust would be hard won he'd also known from the first. Like the flower he'd compared her to, she would close up protectively at the first careless touch.

An engima, his love.

But Travis was patient in spite of—or because of—his love and desire. Instinct told him that when this woman did finally open up to him, he would be glad of his own patience. And if the cost of that patience were to be cold showers and restless nights in a lonely bed, there would be no regrets.

The lover in him might chafe at time wasted, but a deeper part of him knew there was no waste.

Not if she loved him in the end.

The remainder of the afternoon and evening was spent quietly. There was awareness now; Saber could see the warmth in his green eyes and was conscious of his presence, but she was gradually able to relax once more. Except for those fleeting moments of eye-opening shock, as if she'd stepped too close to a fire.

They had dinner at the main house, and the last remnants of tension dissolved in laughter when Cory and Mark joined their table. It was difficult to do anything *but* laugh while the artist was single-mindedly sketching Cory on the back of a menu and she was just as single-mindedly trying to persuade him to eat his dinner; she was finally forced to remove the menu and hand him his fork. Mildly disgruntled, Mark settled down to eat, but not without a pained glance at his patroness that made everyone else laugh.

"He's impossible," Cory told her guests. "The child hasn't the sense to come in out of the rain."

"I'm only a year younger than you," Mark pointed out, unoffended.

Cory rolled her eyes, then grinned. "You'd never know he was twenty-six, would you?"

Travis was surprised and showed it, having long since realized that Mark had no objection to being discussed; he rarely noticed what was said about him and was the most inoffensive young man Travis had ever met. "I would have guessed him younger than that."

Cheerfully, Cory said, "He'll never age. When the rest of us are creaking around in our dotage, he'll look years younger—and act it."

"You'll never be in your dotage," Mark told her. "Bone structure. You'll be elegant, Cory." His perceptive eyes focused across the table at Saber. "And you," he said briskly, "will always be beautiful. I'd like to paint you at eighty," he added.

Travis and Cory were smothering chuckles, but Saber responded gravely, "If we're still around, Mark, you've got a date."

He nodded with such an air of making a mental note to himself that his companions had to laugh yet again. But Mark wasn't finished.

"You'll age well, too," he told Travis with his amiable frankness. "Classic bone structure. You won't even go gray until very late, I think, or wrinkle hardly at all."

"Glad to hear it," Travis managed to say, while the ladies choked into their napkins. "D'you have an inside track we should know about, or is it merely artistic intuition?"

Mark smiled, eating with the methodical gestures of someone simply conforming to society's whims rather than assuaging hunger.

"I think he's psychic," Cory offered. "He can never find his paints, but if anybody else loses something, he can always find it."

"If I were a horse, where would I be?" Mark murmured, still eating.

This baffled his companions for a moment, until Saber laughed suddenly. "I see. That old story about the little boy and the lost horse. He thought to himself, If I were a horse, where would I be?"

"And I went...and I looked...and I was," Mark said placidly.

Cory shook her head at him. "You need a keeper."

"I have one." He smiled at her.

Travis and Saber laughed while Cory choked. "Brat!" she told him.

Mark sighed. "Yes, but what'll I do when your man comes?"

"What man?" she asked, clearly at sea.

"Your man. I imagine he'll be turning up any day now," Mark said, mildly regretful. "But that book'll get you into trouble, and he'll call me a puppy." On this cryptic comment, the artist excused himself and left the table.

Cory stared at her guests. "Sometimes that boy worries me."

"*Is* he psychic?" Saber asked. "All these years and I've never been sure."

Their hostess shrugged. "Beats the hell out of me. Sometimes he says things that sound like nonsense—but I've never known him to miss in eight years."

Saber was amused. "Then I'd say you'd better get ready to meet your destiny."

"Oh, great." Cory sounded a little harassed. "That's all I need right now."

"What book?" Travis asked plaintively.

Cory glared at him. "A stupid book. A *mistake*. And I don't want to talk about it. I'd better go find Mark before he falls down the stairs or something." Regally, she tossed her napkin aside and left the table.

Travis looked at Saber. "What book?"

She smiled. "Well, it's no secret. D'you keep an eye on the bestseller lists?"

"Generally."

"Then maybe you remember a runaway bestseller that hit the top about six months ago—and is still there? *The Art of Courtship?*"

He blinked. "Yes. By . . . C. B. Stewart."

"Cory Briann Stewart," Saber murmured. "It started out as a joke. All her friends come to Cory for romantic advice—men as well as women. Someone told her she should write it all down so they could read her advice instead of pestering her. And she did. As a joke. And—as a joke—one of the friends sent it off to a publisher."

Travis whistled softly. "But the joke was on them."

"I'll say. It's the only time I've ever seen Cory bewildered. She got roped into a promotional tour before she realized. After six weeks of talk shows and the like, she came tearing back here to hide."

Thinking of some of his own experiences, Travis winced. "I can imagine. Stupid questions and sly remarks."

"Oh, yes. Mind you, Cory can take care of herself." Saber grinned suddenly. "They had to bleep her twice on national television! Anyway, after being harassed, scorned, and patronized, not to mention having her personal convictions and opinions belittled, Cory came home."

Travis shook his head sympathetically but said, "I'll have to read it."

"You won't find a copy here. If Cory kept hers, it's under lock and key."

"Did you read it?"

"Of course."

"And?"

"Cory has an instinct about people," Saber said seriously. "And her advice is always sound. The book is generalized, of course, but I'll bet it straightened out more than a few relationships."

"Would it help us?" he asked lightly.

She looked at him for a moment, then smiled. "We don't need the book—we've got Cory."

"Should we ask her advice?" He was still playing it light.

Saber laughed and tossed her napkin aside. "She'll probably advise whether we ask or not. I'm going for a walk; I'll gain ten pounds if I keep eating like this."

"On you," he told her, rising to pull out her chair, "ten pounds would look good. But I'm at the age when I have to be on guard against a spreading middle. Lead the way, ma'am." But he realized she hadn't answered his question.

———

They walked together in silence, listening to the sounds of a warm summer night. It was peaceful and a full moon lighted their way. Eventually, they wound up near the swimming pool, glowing blue from its underwater lights.

"Let's swim," Travis said, looking down at her with a grin.

"In the buff?" she asked dryly.

"Why not? From the sound of it, everyone else's up at the clubhouse." Taking her silence for refusal, he added quickly, "We can go put our suits on."

Saber knew he'd bought a few extra things at the ranch store, including a swimsuit. He'd gone in swimming several mornings, but she had always managed to avoid the pool. Now she strove to keep her voice casual. "Oh, not tonight. I'm ... a little tired."

He took her hand silently as they walked past the pool, and she wondered if he'd noticed how the heel of her hand had rubbed her thigh before she could halt the movement. Stupid habit! She'd have to concentrate, try to realize when she was doing that. But if he hadn't noticed...

He had.

In the cottage, Saber moved restlessly to the radio and turned the dial until she found quiet music, passing two stations playing her own songs in the process. She felt oddly uneasy. There was something about Travis, that same niggling sense of... what? Something—leashed. Banked power. Not necessarily threatening, just elusively *there*. Unnerving. She was aware of his silently watching gaze but managed to ignore it at least partially until he spoke.

"You won't go in swimming," he said quietly. "You never wear shorts in spite of the heat. And on stage, your gowns are long; if there's a slit in the skirt, it's always on the left. Never the right."

Slowly, she moved to curl up in the roomy armchair before meeting his intent eyes. He sat down across from her.

"Is it a scar, Saber?"

She nodded, oddly relieved that he'd guessed.

"You don't limp," he noted.

"No. There was no bone broken, nothing crippling. Just a deep cut."

"Does it . . . still hurt?"

"No."

"Then it's a reminder," he guessed perceptively.

"I suppose plastic surgery could remove it," she said, "but somehow—yes, it is a reminder. It's a battle scar."

He didn't ask what battle had scarred her; he knew that was a question she'd have to answer without being asked. When she was ready. Instead, he said, "I've always thought battle scars were marks of courage. We're too quick these days to remove what we think of as flaws." He stood up suddenly. "I'm going in swimming. Why don't you join me?" Without waiting for a response, he went into his bedroom to change, closing the door behind him.

When he emerged some moments later, he found the living room empty and Saber's bedroom door closed. He hesitated for a moment, then grabbed a large towel from the bathroom and left the cottage. At the deserted pool, he tossed his towel and terry robe over a poolside lounge, stepped out of the light canvas shoes, and dove cleanly into the cool water.

Would she come? Would she trust him to see the battle scar she thought of as a physical flaw? He didn't know. Instinct told him this was a first hurdle in gaining her complete trust. He thought she felt somehow scarred ... more than physically. She had chosen to keep a reminder to be touched unconsciously whenever she was disturbed, which meant she had not yet come to terms with that battle.

He ached at the thought that she'd been hurt so badly. What had she gone through during those missing months? What could have scarred her physically, changed her emotionally? What could have changed a sweet, gentle girl into a taut, guarded woman with a hint of wildness deep in her silvery eyes?

Travis swam methodically, fiercely, needing the release of action. He swam until he was breathless, then floated on his back to recover. After a moment or two, he realized Saber had come.

She stood at the shadowed edge of the pool, the long terry robe she wore a white blur surrounded by dimness. Stood silently. Waiting.

"Come on in," he called casually, shifting positions to tread water. "It feels terrific."

After a long moment, while he watched calmly, she dropped her towel on the lounge beside his, stepped out of her thongs, and untied the sash of her robe. He couldn't see her expression, but her movements were carefully controlled as she tossed the robe aside and stepped to the edge of the pool. Then she dove gracefully into the water.

He remained where he was while she swam the length of the pool before halting, breathless, to tread water a couple of feet away from him.

"You're right. It feels great."

Travis had not looked for the scar, knowing it would be nearly impossible to see in the dimness. And he didn't look now through the lighted blue haze of the water. He just smiled at her. "See what you've been missing?" Without waiting for a response, he challenged, "Race you!"

For nearly an hour they played in the water.

Both were good swimmers, strong and graceful, and they competed in underwater acrobatics as well as in various strokes. Saber forgot her scar as she relaxed, and Travis had the satisfaction of seeing her elusive dimple appear more than once.

Travis was deliberately first out of the water, standing on the tiled side to towel himself dry. "I don't know about you," he said, "but I've had it. Ready to call it a night?"

Saber hesitated, treading water, then took an audible breath and headed for the shallow end. As she climbed the steps leading out of the pool, the moonlight lit what it had only shadowed before. Her black suit gleamed and her skin seemed paler than it actually was. And midway up her right thigh twisted a dark and jagged scar.

It was several inches long, nearly an inch wide, and it was an ugly thing. The only visible mark on her flawless skin, the only imperfection on her beautifully formed body, it was as much a shock as an unexpected physical blow.

Travis looked at that ugliness calmly, feeling

only pain that she'd been hurt that way. He held her towel, reaching to wrap it around her as she halted before him, and the defensive uncertainty in her brilliant eyes wrenched at him. He enfolded her in his arms instinctively, one hand stroking the long wet hair as he held her warmly.

"A diamond is beautiful, flawed or not," he said huskily. "And a beautiful woman is no less lovely for a tiny scar."

"It isn't tiny," she whispered, the damp mat of hair on his chest brushing her cheek and making her skin tingle pleasantly. She felt a sudden peculiar warmth, as though a fire had flared outward from him and was just near enough for her to feel the heat.

He lifted her chin gently. "To me it is. There's so much of you, Saber. So much beauty, so much talent. And, I think—so much courage. What does a scar matter? I love you."

A lonely, needing part of Saber wanted to believe him. But he didn't really know her, and who could love the unknown? Silently, she stepped away from him, using the towel to dry off before shrugging into the robe he held for her. She belted the robe and slid her feet into the thongs as he donned his own robe and shoes, and they made their way from the pool and along the path to their cottage.

SIX

WHEN SABER CAME back into the living room after showering, she found that Travis had completed his own shower and had dressed in pajama bottoms and a light robe. If he noticed she was wearing a short cotton sleepshirt that left the scar exposed, he made no comment, merely asked if she wanted a glass of wine.

"Is there any? I didn't know." Saber curled up in the armchair.

"I had the main house send a couple of bottles,"

he said, handing her a glass of ruby liquid before sitting down across from her. Casually, he added, "You brought a swimsuit along. When did you plan to swim?"

She smiled a little. "Very early or very late. When no one else was around."

Deliberately, he gazed at the scar, now quite visible just below the hem of the sleepshirt. There was a lamp on a table by her chair, and the golden light clearly detailed the jagged mark. Travis wasn't by any means a medical man, but he knew that wound had been left to heal on its own; it had not been stitched. He looked up to see her watching him warily. Solemnly, he said, "I still love you."

Saber smiled in spite of herself, lifting her glass in a tiny toast.

"You're supposed to say you love me, too," he said sternly.

Back on balance, Saber quoted lightly, "'Do not fall in love with me, for I am falser than vows made in wine.' Shakespeare."

"The point's debatable," he said thoughtfully.

"What point?"

"Whether vows made in wine *are* false. Speaking for myself, I keep a clear and honest head until the bitter end."

"You never wake up the morning after the night before with regrets?"

"Never."

"No regrets?" she persisted, amused. "Never even a pained memory of wearing lampshades or teaching the boss's daughter how to tango?"

"I come from an old and honored family," he told her firmly, "and we learned way back to hold our wine well. I could drink the Russian army under the table and still speak a coherent sentence."

Saber wasn't about to confess that wine made *her* reckless to the point of insanity. She glanced at her half-empty glass and made a mental note to be careful; if he kept his head while she lost hers... "Like my father," she murmured without thinking.

"He had a cast-iron stomach, too, huh?"

She looked at him. "Yes."

Travis dismissed the subject. "Well, anyway, we were talking about false vows."

"Were we?"

"I was," he admitted. "I think you were trying to avoid talking about them."

"I brought it up."

"And dropped it in my lap hoping I'd back off. Which, if I were a gentleman, I'd do. Gentlemen never have any fun."

Saber giggled at his disgusted tone.

"However," he added, "since I'm no gentleman, I don't have to let it worry me. *Are* you falser than vows made—whenever?"

"False to the marrow," she said lightly. "You shouldn't believe a word I say."

"Then I won't believe," he murmured, "that you're false to the marrow."

Saber gave him another tiny salute with her glass, then set it to one side. "I'm going to bed." She got to her feet. "It's been a long and strange day."

"Thanks a lot," he said mildly.

She was surprised by an urge to reach out and touch him as she walked around the couch. Surprised and a bit unnerved, because she wasn't a physically demonstrative woman. He *pulled* at her like a magnet. And it wasn't because he was more handsome than any man had a right to be; it was that damned elusive *something*. Thinking about that, she had reached her bedroom door when Travis's voice halted her.

"Saber?"

She turned to find him gazing into his glass, expressionless. "Yes?"

"Those missing months." His voice was neutral. "Did they have anything to do with a man?"

Saber hesitated only a moment. "Not the way you mean. Good night, Travis."

"Good night, Saber." He heard her door close softly. Not the way he meant? Not a lover, then; it was what he meant and they both knew it. But a man had somehow been involved, he thought. Remembering a phone caller she'd refused to identify and weary remarks about "proving" herself to an unidentified "him," Travis stirred restlessly.

Who was he? A part of Saber's past, unquestionably. But what part? Did he belong to the child or the woman? Was he completely of the past or a troubling part of the present?

Not a lover ... but somehow a rival?

Travis felt as if he were deep in a maze without a key. He had the odd feeling, too, that Saber was willing now to tell him about her past. Willing, but somehow unable. As if it were not her secret alone.

Swearing softly, Travis rose and carried both glasses to the kitchen before heading for his bed. He'd gotten involved with Saber in the first place because of questions. Now, with his heart involved, he found the questions getting tougher all the time.

If only he could find a few answers.

Travis woke just after dawn, unable to go back to sleep. He knew by now that Saber usually slept until around nine A.M.—or at least remained in her room until then. To avoid having to find excuses for not swimming with him, he realized now. He enjoyed swimming early in the morning and, restless, he decided to make use of the pool.

The graveled paths were deserted, the silence broken only by the chattering of birds as he made his way to the pool. Alone, he swam for a good hour or more before climbing out to make himself comfortable on one of the lounges. He pulled sunglasses from the pocket of his robe and donned them as the early sunlight glinted harshly off the blue-tinted water. Then he relaxed and blanked his mind, listening to the birds.

It was sometime later when two men came down the path from the main house. The first man to reach the pool was middle-aged, lean, and curiously anonymous; his was a stolid, unremarkable face. He seemed barely to notice Travis, but Travis nonetheless felt he had been weighed and measured in an instant and was now under keen, though inconspicuous, observation.

It puzzled him, but when the second man reached the pool, he understood. The first man was a bodyguard of sorts, because the second man, Travis recognized instantly, was Matt Preston.

Since Travis was interested in larger-than-life personalities, he had heard of the man. Preston was easily one of the richest men in the world; he'd inherited a worldwide conglomerate upon reaching his twenty-first birthday and had spent the past thirty years or so adding steadily to his empire. He was "into" everything: real estate, shipping, manufacturing, electronics, oil, gold, diamonds. He had a fleet of ships the U.S. Navy envied, owned one commercial airline outright and had stock in most of the others, owned property all over the world, and was on a first-name basis with every world-mover of the past few decades.

Uncannily successful in business, his personal history was filled with tragedy. His firstborn son had been kidnapped as an infant, involving law enforcement agencies in a desperate search that had made headlines for months until the child had been found brutally slain; the kidnappers had never been caught. Preston's frail young wife had been shattered, her health nearly destroyed. A second child had been stillborn, and Amy Preston had died giving birth to her third child, a son.

It was said that Matt Preston had been very nearly mad at that point in his life. Cloaking the birth of his son in secrecy, he had refused even to let the public know the name of the child. Using every bit of the considerable influence he had, he made certain that his son could never be a target for kidnappers. No photographs were released, and the boy's nurse shared her duties with a tremendous security staff. During the years that followed, while public curiosity was still strong, not a single fact leaked out about the Preston boy.

Travis had tried to trace the child at one point a few years back but had found absolutely nothing. Even the exact date of birth had been buried too deeply to be found. Those closest to Preston, friends and employees, were incredibly loyal and amazingly silent.

Now, watching the lean man as he discarded his robe and dove into the pool, Travis found himself wondering about Matt Preston's son. Where was he now? He was beyond school age and presumably led a life of some sort—but what kind of life? Preston had never remarried, throwing himself into his financial empire to the exclusion of all else. Did he even see his son?

With sunglasses hiding his interest, Travis studied Preston. A tall man, lean and hard-muscled, he had thick silver hair and rapier-keen blue eyes. His face was an expressionless mask, but filled with character and almost unlined. He looked the hard man his life had made him, but Travis knew he supported countless charities and was known to possess an almost compulsive interest in the welfare of children; rumor had it that the only thing holding the power to enrage him was neglect or abuse of a child—any child.

Travis was pulled from thought as Cory approached the pool, stunning in a black bikini that turned the heads of all three men. Even the bodyguard, Travis noted with suppressed amusement, allowed his mouth to fall open briefly.

"Oh, damn," Cory said, surveying her guests with disfavor, "I thought the pool would be deserted this early."

Travis, closest to her, pulled his sunglasses down his nose and peered at her. "Are you planning to *swim* in that?" he asked politely.

She lifted an eyebrow. "It's anchored more securely than it appears to be.

"It'd have to be to swim in," he agreed.

Matt Preston pulled himself up the ladder and accepted the towel his bodyguard tossed to him. "Morning, Cory," he greeted, the icy eyes warming and a smile curving his mouth.

"Matt." She nodded to the bodyguard. "Hi, Alex."

"Good morning, Cory." The bodyguard's voice was deep and even.

"Have you three met?" Without waiting for an answer, she cheerfully introduced the men before tossing her towel aside and stepping down into the shallow end of the pool. The men made polite noises at each other, then the bodyguard went back to his book as Matt sat down in a lounge beside Travis.

In spite of his expressionless face, Matt Preston turned out to be a very charming man. He seemed very much at ease, asking Travis about several of his books that he'd obviously read. They talked while Cory swam energetically in the pool, both turning their attention to her as she climbed out and grabbed her towel.

Sinking down in the third lounge chair, Cory

smiled at both men. "Matt, I told Mark you'd gotten in late last night. He went off to paint the dawn or something."

Matt's face softened. "I'm glad he's here."

Suddenly alert. Travis watched the older man covertly. Was *that* it? Could the vague, artistic Mark possibly be Matt Preston's son? Had Matt Preston continued to protect his son as an adult when it became obvious he was totally unsuited for the business world? Difficult, he thought, to find a resemblance between Matt's hard face and Mark's amiable features—but they both had blue eyes, and Mark was the right age....

Then Travis's thoughts were yanked from the artist when Matt spoke again. His face had gone expressionless, eyes hooded as he gazed at Cory.

"Did you tell Saber I was here?" he asked quietly.

"Uh—no." Cory shot a quick, uncomfortable look at Travis. "I haven't seen her this morning."

Matt gave an odd, twisted smile but said nothing.

Travis gazed steadily at Cory, who refused to

meet his eyes. He felt suspended thoughts crashing in his mind. Matt Preston—and Saber? No. No, she'd said ... Then he remembered Saber had denied only that a lover had been involved in the months missing from her life. But there was still the man she had to prove something to, the man for whom her success meant too much.

Numbly, Travis knew that Saber was not a woman who would accept a rich lover or husband as her due; she would strive to stand on equal terms with a man. Granted, she would never be as rich as Matt Preston, but she could very well be as successful. And Preston ...

Travis tried to look at the man objectively. Handsome, distinguished, incredibly wealthy— and not much past fifty. He could have any woman he wanted. And if he wanted Saber? Was he waiting patiently for her to prove she didn't need the riches he offered—before laying them at her feet?

Travis barely heard the older man excuse himself before going over to talk to his bodyguard. But he watched the graceful, athletic stride, tearing his brooding gaze away only when Cory claimed his attention.

"Travis?"

He turned his head to find her watching him with sympathy in her green eyes. "Travis, trust Saber," she said softly.

"I want to." He heard the rough emotion in his voice and didn't try to hide it. "But she won't tell me anything. How can I accept her past as unimportant when she won't trust me enough to confide in me?"

"Maybe it isn't a matter of trust," Cory suggested. "Saber hasn't had an easy life, Travis. You've guessed that?"

He nodded.

Cory seemed to be weighing her words carefully. "She's been . . . cheated in a lot of ways. She has incredible courage, more than she realizes. But there are debts and promises in her past, and they have to be dealt with."

"If I lose her to him—" Travis grated out, shooting a glance toward Matt and not finishing the savage sentence.

Biting her lip, Cory stared at him worriedly. "Travis, Saber needs you. She needs someone who loves her for what she is—not because she's beautiful and famous. She needs an anchor. A person with a special kind of strength."

"A hero?" he suggested wryly, thinking of that larger-than-life part of her.

"In a way, yes. Not a doer of great deeds, though." Cory smiled. "I think you'll find that Saber's definition of a hero is something entirely different. Ask her sometime. You may be surprised."

Travis nodded, then rose abruptly and shrugged into his robe. "I'll tell her Preston's here." He managed a smile for Cory's anxious eyes, then left the pool and made his way to their cottage.

Saber was in the kitchen, busy making pancakes, and Travis only greeted her lightly before going into his bedroom to change. When he came out and joined her, she had set the small table for two and was pouring coffee.

"Hope you're hungry," she said cheerfully. "I got carried away and made lots of pancakes."

"Starved." Travis thought that he carried off this carefree routine pretty well—until she spoke about ten minutes into the meal.

"What's wrong, Travis?"

After a moment, he said casually, "Cory introduced me to two new guests out at the pool."

"Oh?"

"Yes." He sipped his coffee as he watched her finishing her meal. "One was Alex—didn't catch his last name. The other was Matt Preston." Her face did a fine job of hiding whatever she felt, he thought, but there was dismay in the quick glance she threw him. Evenly, he added, "He asked Cory if she'd told you he was here."

Saber pushed the food around on her plate for several moments, then lifted her eyes to meet his.

Gazing into the serene, unreadable silver eyes, Travis was unable to stop the words escaping from the very heart of him. "Is he the man, Saber? Is he the one you have to prove something to?"

"Yes," she said steadily.

"You're in love with him," he said.

Something flickered in her eyes, then vanished. "No. But I love him."

Travis put his napkin aside and rose to his feet in the very controlled motion of a man who had to *move* or do something violent. He left the kitchen, pacing the larger space of the living room.

Saber followed him, watching him silently. When she finally spoke, it was in an oddly anguished voice. "Travis, there are things I can't explain to you right now. I made a promise, and until I'm freed of it . . ."

"You can't tell me why Matt Preston's important to you?"

"No," she said, badly unnerved. He was pacing like a tiger in a cage, and she wondered dimly why until now she had seen only that rare surface beauty. Why she had glimpsed only the rippling muscles and deadly grace of a vital primitive creature? She was not frightened, but something inside her was awed, made wary and uncertain.

He stopped pacing, gazing across the room at her. It was her vulnerability that reached through the fog of his painful jealousy.

"I love you," he said huskily. Swiftly, he moved to stand before her. "And I'll fight for you. But I have to know what I'm fighting, Saber."

"You're not fighting Matt," she whispered.

He reached out to enfold her in his arms, holding her tightly. "I've never been jealous before," he said. "I don't . . . quite know how to handle it."

Saber burrowed closer to him, obeying a sudden need for the touch of him, the feeling of his hard body pressed to hers. There was an unfamiliar ache in the pit of her belly, a hollow longing she'd never known before. Disturbed, she tried to keep her mind on his words.

"Give me time," she murmured.

He framed her face in warm hands, turning it up so that she could see the tenderness in his green eyes. "We'll take all the time you need," he said gently.

Saber gazed up at him for a long moment, then said quietly, "There is something I want to tell you about now."

Travis watched the lovely, delicate face tighten, felt tension flow into stiffening shoulders. Silently he led her to the couch and sat beside her. "Then tell me," he said.

So she did, her voice level and calm, her silver-gray eyes flickering from time to time with the caged wildness that had fascinated him from the beginning. She talked about the months missing from her life, and a battle that had scarred her physically and wrenched a woman from a girl.

A battle of survival . . . and she lived it again.

It had been a freak accident, a combination of violent storm and the failure of delicate instruments. The chances of her surviving the crash had been a million to one. And the odds against her continued survival—alone, lost, too many miles from civilization, and in a hostile, unfamiliar environment—had been astronomical.

She was a delicate creature with no experience of physical or emotional hardships. Educated for city streets and dinner parties. Accustomed to soft beds and clean clothes and processed foods. She had never before seen violent death or wilderness or her own blood.

Now, as the midday sun glinted off twisted, ugly chunks of metal, she tied an awkward knot in the strip of material torn from a silk blouse. Blank gray eyes stared at the improvised bandage covering the jagged cut on her thigh. She'd been unable to find the first-aid kit in the Lear; there was so little left. And the cockpit...

She didn't look toward the ungodly tangle of fuselage and trailing wires that had held the controls of the jet and was now a tomb for the two men within it. She had shared two nights and two days with the dead men and the dead jet, clinging numbly to the vague understanding that she was supposed to remain at the crash site and await rescue.

Her shocked gray eyes combed the sky constantly, endlessly; her ears strained to catch the comforting throb of engines. Nothing.

It came to her slowly, reluctantly, finally, that no one was coming.

There was no one to help her.

No one to tell her what to do.

The storm that had beaten them to the ground had first driven them far off course, crippling the delicate instruments that should have told them where they were.

Lost. And alone for the first time in her life.

She unfolded a grimy handkerchief and slowly chewed the last of the berries she'd found near the jet. They did little to ease the empty ache in her stomach. Then she picked up the backpack she'd improvised from bits of salvaged clothing and slung it over one shoulder. She gained her feet, leaning awkwardly on the slender, strong branch of a tree she'd found; it was hardly a comfortable crutch, but at least it braced her weak, throbbing right leg.

What little food there'd been on the jet had not survived in an edible condition. There'd been nothing to carry water in except a Thermos, and it was empty; she'd stuck it in the backpack. She had taken three small bottles of liquor that had miraculously survived the crash unbroken; the fourth she had poured on her thigh to splash agony on the raw, jagged flesh.

Planning to do some hiking, she had at least packed comfortable boots, and she had a broad-brimmed hat. She had cut her jeans off at the thighs because of the wound, and found a torn but relatively intact, overlarge cotton shirt that had once been sleepwear.

She had a penknife she always carried because her father had given it to her years before. And she had found a couple of very dull knives among the scattered remains of the Lear's galley cutlery.

Not much. Not much at all to spell the difference between survival and a lonely, agonizing death.

Hobbling painfully, she turned away from the crashed jet.

North. For want of a better choice. It was, at least for a while, downhill. She had carefully calculated the direction this morning, finding east when the sun rose and hoping she was right. She had reason now to be thankful for a lifelong habit of reading; among others, she'd read a great many "how-to" books and was especially grateful for those titles that had seemed merely ironic and amusing, considering her sheltered life-style: *How to Live Off the Land; How to Cook Over an Open Fire; How Not to Be Lost in the Woods*... and others. So amusing then.

So vitally important now.

She wished she had been a Girl Scout....

SEVEN

SABER TOLD HIM everything. She told him of those first days when, weakened by hunger and pain, she'd very nearly died. She told him of the desperate search for water, for food. She talked distantly of mountains, forests, lakes, loneliness. Of learning to hunt and fish, and read the signs of coming weather.

She didn't look at him, but into the past.

"I found later that countless times I'd barely missed people. It was hard to travel in a straight line because of the terrain; I'd have to walk south for a day, or follow a meandering stream. When I tried to chart my journey later, I saw that at times I'd been just a mountain away from a town.

"A part of me wanted to give up at first. And I think...that part of me died. I can remember when it happened. It was the fifth or sixth day, and I hadn't had anything to eat. I was trying to catch a tiny fish in a stream with my hands. But it moved so quickly and I was awkward and weak. Then— somehow—I was looking down at that fish on the bank, and I felt suddenly strong. I *knew* then I was going to make it."

She dropped her eyes to the strong hand holding her own; it was white-knuckled with tension, but gentle in its touch. Meeting his gaze for the first time since she'd begun talking, she wondered at the oddly blurred look of his green eyes, the pallor beneath his tan. But he said nothing, and she went on.

"You wondered if I was the same singer who recorded two years ago; I'm not. That girl, that weak girl. She didn't know how to live. So she curled up inside herself and didn't exist anymore."

She sighed, a breath of sound. "Once I'd learned how to survive, I was—well, proud. After a while, I learned to enjoy being alone. Really alone. The world seemed so new and fascinating. The last few months, I even avoided people once I'd found them. I just wandered."

Travis stared at her. He wasn't aware of holding his breath as he gazed into those silvery eyes, as he saw what she'd kept carefully hidden until now. Behind the glaze of intelligent serenity lay the explosive power she allowed to escape only on stage, the almost primitive, driven strength that had enabled her to survive when she should have died.

"You made it," Travis said softly, saluting her courage. "No one helped you. No one told you what to do. A devastating crash, a terrible injury, and nothing but your hands and your wits—and you *survived*. You survived alone and, instead of losing yourself, you found yourself. The hothouse flower grew and flourished under the most hostile conditions possible."

"Did I find myself?" she asked, eyes flickering. "Or . . . lost part of myself? I . . . I regret what I lost, Travis. But I can't regret what I found. I never knew until then how badly I wanted to live. I never knew I was strong enough to live like that."

"Larger than life. No wonder your voice changed," he said slowly. "Everything but strength and determination was stripped away from you."

"But is that all that's left?" Saber gazed up at him, troubled. "It used to be easier to laugh. And to cry. It used to be easier to . . . do what was expected of me. I never had to wonder about my place in the scheme of things. Now I wonder if the best part of me was destroyed during those months."

"No," he said flatly.

Saber smiled. "You never knew me before."

"I saw the pictures," he said. "Heard the voice. That girl was a gentle, fragile creature, with no power, no passion in her voice. But you—you have the gentleness; it's in your eyes, your soft voice.

And when you sing, that passionate part of you is released." He looked at her steadily. "That's what puzzled me about you from the beginning. Onstage, you are explosive, powerful. You reach out and grip the hearts of thousands of people. But why . . . only onstage, Saber? Why do you hide that part of yourself the rest of the time?"

She turned her eyes away from him, gazing into distance and time, or perhaps another life; she was too far away for him even to guess where she was.

"I . . . When I got back, there were—people— who were troubled by what I'd become. People who regretted the loss of that girl. It seemed there was suddenly . . . too much of me." Saber shook her head, blinking away those disturbing thoughts and meeting his eyes again. "Onstage, it seems right," she finished simply.

Travis, listening, was suddenly aware of a yearning ache within him. Though he had seen both, he had yet to hold either Saber within his heart and his arms. Instinct told him Matt Preston

was the "people" troubled by Saber's metamor-
phosis, and that she had tried to find a bridge link-
ing those two parts of her. Neither one nor the
other, strength disguised as stage presence and vulnerability masked by control.

What had her manager said? That...at best her
energy was an illusion and at worst a shield? That
offstage she caged the jungle-cat wildness and hid
behind the bars....A perceptive man, Travis
thought. But not entirely correct.

The stage presence was the reality; it was the
cage that was a manufactured illusion.

Travis suddenly lifted her hand to his lips. "One
day," he said, "I hope you'll realize you never have
to hide anything from me. There could never be...
too much of you."

She looked at him, her silvery eyes puzzled.
"How can you be so sure?" she asked, the vulnerability peeking through. "Why is it that you...seem
to understand me? Without *knowing* me?"

"I love you," he replied.

After a moment, Saber gently pulled her hand
from his grasp and rose to pace the room. She

seemed distracted, troubled. "I just wanted to be free," she murmured as if to herself. "But now I don't know—" Suddenly she faced him, her eyes focusing on him. "I think I'll go for a walk, Travis. D'you mind?"

"No," he said quietly. There was nothing else he could say.

"It may be a long walk," she warned, averting her eyes.

"All right."

Travis watched her leave the cottage, a sick feeling of dread tightening in his chest. She would see Matt Preston, and he knew it.

He thought of the elusive parts of Saber, wondered dimly if he were trying to chain lightning. Was he strong enough to hold such an explosive, elemental force?

Was Matt Preston?

Swearing softly, Travis left the cottage.

Travis played a few sets of tennis with one of the other guests—who turned out to be a U.S. senator—and won every game. Then, after showering and changing, he went up to the main house for lunch.

He found the artist.

And Matt Preston.

They were sitting together at a table near the big bay window in the dining room. Mark talking and Preston listening with a faint smile. Travis wasn't very interested in what they were saying; their relationship seemed unimportant now.

He made his way to the table where Cory sat, eating absently while she frowned down at a sheaf of papers.

"Cory—"

She looked up, still frowning. "Linens," she said darkly. "The prices are outrageous, and we *have* to have them, after all."

"Cory, have you seen Saber?"

The redhead nodded. "Sure. She had the cook fix her a picnic lunch and went off with it a couple of hours ago."

"Oh." Travis glanced toward Preston, wondering if Saber had seen him yet. He was distracted when a waitress came to the table to take his order and automatically sat down across from Cory as he told the girl what he wanted for lunch. Not that he wanted anything, really.

When the waitress had gone, Cory said calmly, "Your face is an open book, my friend."

Travis had realized that Cory was the type of woman people *talked* to. The green eyes were warmly interested in everything, and she had the rare gift of being able to listen. He thought fleetingly that she probably knew secrets worth a fortune.

"Is it?" he asked lightly.

"War and Peace," she said, equally light.

He abandoned the pretense. "I've never before wanted something I couldn't fight for."

Cory seemed mildly surprised. "You can fight for Saber?"

"How?" he demanded. "She wants time—I'm trying to give her what she wants. She tells me there are things she can't discuss—I'm not asking."

"In fact," Cory said politely, "you're being very patient and considerate."

Stung by the faintly derisive gleam he caught in her eyes, Travis snapped, "What else should I be?" He sat back to allow the waitress to set his plate before him, then attacked the food, wishing it were something else.

Cory was studying her iced tea with a reflective air. "Oh, I'm sure you're doing the right thing, Travis," she said. "Patience is a very endearing trait."

"I don't want to lose her," he muttered.

"Of course not," she said in a soothing tone.

Travis carefully laid aside his fork. "Will you *stop* agreeing with me," he said through his teeth, "and tell me what to do?"

"What d'you want to do, Travis?" she asked.

"I want to carry her off to our cottage and—"

"I think I can fill in the blanks." Cory gazed at him, smiling sweetly. "So what's stopping you?"

"I don't want to—"

"Frighten her? She's a grown woman, you

know. Of course, it might *startle* her just a bit. Since you've been so forbearing, I mean. When one gets accustomed to being treated a certain way— after asking for that treatment, mind you—sometimes it's the very devil of a problem to straighten out." Cory gazed into space, musing.

He stared at her. "But if she's not sure, and I push her—"

"Who said anything about pushing her? We were talking about filling in the blanks. And fighting for what one wants."

"That isn't pushing?"

"Travis," she said in a courteous tone, "there is a vast difference between a caveman and a lover. And if you don't know that at your age, there's no hope for you."

Unwillingly, he began to smile. "No wonder your book sold like hotcakes," he murmured.

Cory gathered up her papers. "Never mind my book," she said sternly. "We were discussing your anemic love life."

"Not anemic!" he protested indignantly.

"Oh, really? My dear man, how d'you expect

Saber to know what she wants when she's never *had* it? Your job is to make very certain she knows what she has been and would be missing," Cory told him. "And if you can't handle that—"

"I can," he interrupted hastily.

Cory rose to her feet and looked down her nose at him. "We'll see. Now, if you'll excuse me, I have to go and order some ridiculously expensive linens."

"Cory?" he said before she could turn away.

"Yes?"

"Thanks."

Green eyes gleamed at him briefly. "Don't mention it." Then she was threading her way among the tables in the dining room.

Travis found he was hungry after all.

And impatient to find Saber.

Travis's impatience grew as the day lengthened. After several hours of wandering around the grounds, he sought Cory, who was on the phone at the front desk in the main house. Judging by her exasperated expression and silence, she was on "hold" and not too pleased about it.

She dangled the receiver in one hand as Travis approached, saying irritably, "There's something depressing about canned music while you wait."

"Have you seen Saber?"

"You have a one-track mind."

"Cory."

She sighed. "She returned the picnic basket about an hour ago, then went back out. I don't know where she is."

"I'll find her," he said, turning away.

"Well, if you don't find her immediately," Cory called after him plaintively, "would you please contain your panthering? You've made three of my other guests nervous."

He lifted a hand in acknowledgment as he left the house, wondering if his impatient wanderings were really disturbing anyone. Not that he cared; he just wanted to find Saber.

The only measure of comfort he found during the long afternoon was that Saber was not with Matt Preston. The billionaire remained in plain view all the time, posing for Mark's eager sketching as they sat near a whitewashed fence to the left of the main house.

As a last resort, Travis followed the path Saber had taken the day before. The sun was going down when he finally admitted defeat and made his way past the house and toward the cottage paths. Absently he noted that artist and subject had decided to call it a day and that the grounds were nearly deserted; the guests were probably getting ready for dinner.

The discreet shrubbery lighting had not yet come on, and the path was dim, but Travis had no difficulty making out the two people standing before the cottage he shared with Saber. He stopped in his tracks, unnoticed by either of them. Good manners might have demanded that he announce his presence or else go away: he did neither.

And he was close enough to hear as well as see.

"I had no choice," Matt Preston said, his face oddly set.

"You had no right!" Saber responded in a low, angry voice.

"Didn't I?"

Preston's next words were too low for Travis to catch, and Saber's voice had fallen to a furious whisper. It was a quick, harsh exchange, ending when Preston's face seemed to quiver as if from a blow and Saber reached out to touch his arm.

Travis was vaguely aware of his hands curling into fists. For long moments he heard no more than the murmur of their voices, calmer now. Then Preston bent to kiss her lightly. "Thank you, honey."

"Good night, Matt."

Saber stood and watched as he made his way along one of the many paths leading to the main house. When he was lost from sight, she turned and went into the cottage, closing the door behind her.

Travis stood where he was for endless minutes, staring at the golden light spilling from the cottage. The conversation he'd seen and heard filled his mind with ghostly echoes; his instincts told him he'd *know* what it all meant if he could only think.

There was something just beyond his grasp, some scrap of knowledge he held without realizing.

But he couldn't think; he could only feel. His love for Saber was like the wildness in her silvery eyes—caged by caution and patience. But in that moment what was caged became stronger than the bars and burst free with an abrupt, savage need.

Primitive instinct drove him to fight for what he wanted, to reach out and grasp what he needed with all the strength he could command. Caveman and lover fought wildly as he strode toward the cottage.

And it was a toss-up as to which won.

Saber jumped in surprise when the cottage door slammed violently, turning from the radio she'd just switched on to stare toward the sound. Travis stood in the shadows by the door, and she felt weak with relief.

"Lord, you scared me half to death," she said.

He was silent, motionless; she couldn't make out his expression.

"Travis?" She thought she knew what was wrong. "I'm sorry for disappearing all day." She was still torn between excitement and alarm after realizing sometime during the day that she was head over heels in love with him. Would he walk away from her when he learned the truth? And could she blame him if he did? "Cory said you'd been looking for me."

"Yes, I have." His voice was calm, conversational.

Relief flooded her a second time. Surely he couldn't be angry? Not when he sounded so calm. "I *am* sorry, but I warned you about that habit of mine. Was there ... was there anything special you wanted me for?"

"Yes, there was something special." He came forward slowly into the light.

Saber felt the breath catch in her throat. His green eyes were blazing with a light she'd never seen before, hot and shimmering. His lean, handsome face was rigid, almost masklike, and he was moving with the restrained steadiness of leashed emotion.

"Travis?"

"I've been very patient," he said evenly, still coming toward her with that careful control.

Saber swallowed hard, fighting an urge to back away. "Travis, what's wrong with you?"

"You agree I've been patient?" he said in the tone of a man who means to be understood clearly.

"Yes—yes, of course you have."

He nodded in a measured way. "There are limits to patience, Saber."

Saber felt hypnotized, her eyes fixed on him as he came nearer. Nearer. By the time he stood before her, she was finding it difficult to breathe and couldn't tear her gaze from the shimmering intensity of those green eyes. "Travis?" she whispered, realizing belatedly that his quiet patience had been deceptive, to say the least.

This was no civilized man, loving in his words and tender in his actions; this was a man with pagan drums beating in his breast, driven by an overwhelming need.

Travis reached out abruptly and hauled her into his arms. "I love you!" he said fiercely, and covered her lips with his.

Like a match set to dry kindling, Saber instantly took fire. There was no slow building of passion, no gradual awareness of desire. She had no time, no opportunity to control the surging release of shatteringly powerful emotions; something broke with a shudder that rocked her entire body and sent her mind reeling helplessly.

The elemental wildness rose up in triumph to meet his equally savage need, fire meeting fire in a crucible's white-hot fury. If she'd been granted a single instant's realization, Saber would have dragged that wild part of her back into hiding: it was meant to be flung only into battling for survival—or into an audience of thousands where it would not overpower. But Travis gave her no time to hesitate, no chance to doubt.

She was lifted into his hard arms, carried to a

bed lit by the faint gleam of the living room lamps. Only dimly aware of being set once more on her feet, she felt his hands coping feverishly with the buttons of her blouse. Her own fingers sought him blindly, parting buttons to find the hard-muscled chest beneath, the texture of curling hair a sensation she craved. She kicked sandals aside, lowered her arms briefly to permit the passing of her blouse and lace bra, both of which were ruined in his fevered haste.

His own shirt fell to the floor and shoes went spinning into a corner unheeded. Burning lips trailed hungry kisses down her throat, and his hands lifted to surround the aching weight of her breasts.

Saber moaned low in her throat, holding his dark head with both her hands as she felt the sudden pull of his mouth, the rough brush of his tongue swirling erotically. Her fingers threaded through his thick hair as his hands spanned her waist, his mouth moved lower. Her jeans were unfastened and slid down over her hips and legs until she could automatically step out of them; silken panties followed.

As he straightened, her hands moved downward over powerful shoulders, over the muscled chest that was rising and falling rapidly; she felt his flat stomach tauten at her touch, felt his breath catch as she found the fastening of his jeans.

Green eyes flashing with emerald fire, he stared down at her, saw her as she'd never been seen before. His hands tangled in her long hair and his mouth found hers again.

Blindly, she pushed the jeans down over his narrow hips. She felt him kick the last of his clothing aside, heard the sound he made as he lifted her and lay her on the bed in a single motion. Then he was beside her, his hands caressing with unsteady need, his mouth hot and demanding.

Saber couldn't breathe and didn't care. She ached; her whole body throbbed with needing him. Hunger sent her hands exploring, all her senses vibrantly alive to the feeling of his body beneath her touch. The painful need of her own body intensified, became a tortured ache, a punishing demand.

She heard a voice that was vulnerable in its yearning, wild in its hunger, and only dimly recognized it as her own. She didn't know what she asked, but he answered. His body moved over hers, taut with savage desire, feverish with the towering flame they had set alight.

Her body instinctively fit itself to cradle his, and when he moved suddenly she cried out, taking as fiercely as she gave. She held him with every part of herself, her grace and strength meeting his in an explosion that rocked them both. They rose together, higher and higher, tension building, splintering, dissolving in a firestorm of sheer boundless pleasure....

For a long time there was only the sound of harsh breathing and pounding hearts, only a trembling aftermath too precious to disturb. They clung to each other, silent and awed.

Finally, Travis turned her chin up with a gentle

hand and gazed into smoky gray eyes now oddly shy. "Dear God, I love you," he said, his voice low and husky.

"I love you, too," she replied.

He caught his breath, released it in a ragged sigh. "You're . . . sure? I don't think I could stand it if you weren't sure."

Saber traced the line of his jaw with a single unsteady finger. "I'm very sure." She smiled slowly. "I was sure even before your patience ran out."

"I won't apologize for that," he murmured, his arms tightening around her. "For the first time, you didn't hide anything from me. Lord, Saber, I've never felt anything like that in my life. And when I realized . . . you never had, either . . . I couldn't believe it."

Her mouth twisted in a wry little smile, but the silvery eyes were alight with laughter. "Thanks a lot."

"You're so beautiful. Have all the men you've known been blind and stupid?" He thought fleetingly of Preston but dismissed the thought; the very fact that no other man had known her explosive passion told him that Preston was not a rival in that way.

"All the men I've known..." Saber gave an odd laugh. "It never mattered before, Travis. This time it mattered."

"Because you love me?"

"Because I love you."

EIGHT

"IT TOOK YOU long enough," he murmured.

Her eyes gleamed. "I could say the same for you."

Travis chuckled. "We'll both have to thank Cory."

"She told you to—?"

"More or less. Actually, she just made a suggestion I was longing for anyway." His hand slid down over her curved hip to the jagged scar on her thigh. "I didn't need much prompting."

She didn't stiffen, but he could feel her awareness of where his hand was, and he went on calmly. "Maybe Cory realized that you could never really be sure about me until you ... let yourself go."

"Is that what I did?" she asked uncertainly.

Travis gazed at her, his face tender. "Darling, you were wonderful. I thought I'd die with needing you, and you were so passionate, so strong. It was as if I held lightning in my arms."

"I ... I lost control," she admitted, her eyes still searching his.

"I hope you'll always lose control with me," he said steadily. "It tore me to pieces inside to hear what you'd gone through after the crash, but I love the part of you that came alive in that hell. The courage. The incredible force you release onstage ... and while loving me."

Her gaze fell before his, and there were misgivings in the vulnerable curve of her lips. "After the crash, I needed that—that wildness to survive. And it seemed right then. But when I came home, those strong feelings frightened me and sometimes unnerved other people. Onstage, I was reaching out to thousands, and that wildness just came out."

"But you hid it offstage," he finished quietly. "That's why you didn't try to have the scar removed, isn't it? It was a reminder to you not to let that amazing strength escape, because you were afraid it would overpower others."

"It didn't overpower you," she ventured.

Quietly, he admitted, "I wasn't sure I could hold that vital part of you. I only knew that I wanted it, needed it. And it was like..." His voice trailed off for a moment, his eyes darkening. "Like skydiving...or walking a highwire...or daring the eye of a hurricane. I've never felt so completely exhilarated in my life."

Saber released a sigh. "I felt that way," she said unevenly. "And I thought you did, too. But I wasn't sure."

"You can be very sure, darling." His arms shifted their hold, pulling her on top of him. "In fact"—green eyes shimmering with a growing intensity—"I think I'd like to dare the eye of a hurricane... again."

"You'll need something to hold on to," she reminded him, breathless.

"I'll hold the lightning," he whispered.

And he did.

"You know, you're larger than life yourself," Saber said thoughtfully sometime later. They had shared a shower before dressing, she in a caftan and he in a robe. They had called to the main house for dinner to be sent and were now halfway through the meal.

Travis was surprised. "Who—me? I'm just an observer, sweetheart."

"You didn't seem to be doing much observing a little while ago," she murmured.

"Somebody to hold the lightning," he said, pretending to be wounded.

Saber smiled but refused to be distracted. "Think about it, Travis. I remember you told me that heroic people fascinated you, and that it was *people* you wanted to write about. How they got where they are, and what it took to become powerful in some way. I've read your books, and your insight into that struggle for success is amazing."

"Thank you, ma'am. And so?"

"And so ... how could you have the insight to understand that struggle? It's easy to understand surface motivations, but you go so much deeper than that. And another thing." She gazed at him reflectively. "In case you hadn't realized it, you're just a little too good to be true."

Travis had to laugh at her tone. "Music to my ears," he said cheerfully. "Play more, darling."

"Well, dammit—you're too good-looking, for one thing."

He was aware that women found him attractive, but Saber's plaintive accusation tickled his sense of humor. "Now *that*'s the pot calling the kettle black with a vengeance. According to all the studies, men tend to find very beautiful women threatening— and you are certainly very beautiful."

Saber accepted the compliment matter-of-factly, even though hers was not the style of beauty she personally admired. "Yes, but that's not what I meant exactly."

"What did you mean?"

She thought for a moment, frowning, somehow convinced that the point was important. "Well, whenever someone describes me in glowing terms, they're always talking about the stage presence. But when they meet me *offstage,* the description is totally different; they say I'm small, I'm slight, I'm fragile. They describe me as *less* offstage, and *more* onstage."

"Because that's when you're most powerful," he agreed, adding. "They see the lightning—but they can't touch it."

Saber nodded. "But with *you* . . . they touch the lightning without knowing what it is."

He blinked. "They do?"

"I did." She gestured slightly. "From the first moment we met, I felt the force of your personality. It wasn't a physical or mental attraction: that came a little later. I thought, Now, *there's* a handsome man. But something about you made me wary. It was like . . . like looking at a quiet volcano and *knowing* somehow that it was about to erupt."

Travis blinked again. "Good Lord."

She grinned at him. "Well, it was. I mean, you were very calm and patient, but I kept thinking things like 'still waters run deep' and 'ninety-something percent of an iceberg is below the surface.' I had the peculiar feeling that my nice gentle tiger went out and ate people at night."

He burst out laughing again. "Oh, no! My poor darling, no wonder you were wary."

Saber was still smiling. "And the more I thought about it, the more confused I became. There you were, soft-spoken and gentle and patient. A paragon of all the virtues, in fact. You slid effortlessly into my life and I could never quite figure out how you managed to get in under my guard. I...I have a pretty strong guard. But you got in somehow. You didn't demand—you asked. Politely. But it was unnerving to keep getting images of an iron hand in a velvet glove. A couple of times I was almost tempted to do something rash— order you to get the hell out of my life or something. Just to see what'd happen."

"But?" He was grinning.

Sheepishly, she admitted, "But it's not safe to

watch a volcano erupt while standing on the slopes of the thing." When he chuckled, Saber went on, "D'you see what I meant by saying you're larger than life? You say you saw something elusive in me, something I released onstage; I *felt* something in you, and I was afraid it was something I couldn't control."

"You should have turned your lightning loose on my tiger in the beginning; think of the time we'd have saved! Like I said—I was a little worried that the vital part of *you* was something I couldn't hold."

Saber frowned a little. "Yes, but I never equated the two. What I felt in you was . . . strength and power. What I was afraid of in myself was wildness. I kept having the uncomfortable feeling that I'd reverted or something after the crash. And I guess I did; God knows I survived more by instinct than knowledge."

"Yet you thought of me as a people-eating tiger," he reminded her, amused. "If that isn't wild, I don't know what is!"

"True." Saber laughed. "I suppose I just wasn't thinking clearly."

"I'll go along with that," Travis said cheerfully, tossing his napkin aside. "Because if you'd been thinking clearly, darling, you would have fallen instantly in love with my too handsome face and manly form, instead of waiting 'a little later' for that."

"Travis?" She was trying not to laugh. "What're you doing?"

What he was doing was picking up her bodily from her chair and striding toward the bedroom. "It's going to storm," he told her amiably. "You should always get under cover before a storm."

Saber felt the strength and grace of a tiger's vital muscles holding her effortlessly and looked into green eyes bright with a kindling fire. She linked her fingers together within the thick black hair. "I guess . . . tigers like storms," she murmured breathlessly.

"This one loves the lightning."

He kicked the bedroom door shut behind them.

———

Sleepily, Saber murmured. "His tiger's heart wrapped in a beautiful soft skin..."

Travis yawned and pulled her even closer to his side. "Quoting somebody?" he inquired.

"Paraphrasing." She paused, trying to remember the source. "Greene. Robert Greene. But *his* tiger's heart was wrapped in a player's hide. I think. Anyway, you're no shabby tiger. That's from somebody else."

He chuckled. "You're not making much sense, darling. Still, you do pretty well for bottled lightning."

"Is that what I am?"

"Certainly. Although the quote I had in mind is in a totally wrong context. 'Bring in the bottled lightning, a tumbler, and a corkscrew.' Dickens."

She giggled. "That kind of bottled lightning, huh? I thought you never got drunk."

Mildly surprised, Travis said, "I guess it does fit, after all. You're the only kind of bottled lightning I get drunk on, sweetheart."

"I think I like that."

"I know I do."

More than half-asleep, she added, "Good thing I don't get drunk on tigers. I do crazy things when I drink too much."

"Such as?"

But she was asleep, and Travis laughed softly to himself.

The following day was something of a fascinating revelation for Travis. He had called Saber a touch-me-not flower, wary, protective; he had known and embraced the elemental lightning that had saved her life and rocketed her to stardom as a performer; he had seen fleeting moments of the fragility captured in a studio photo two years before.

What he saw now was a gradual blending of the three. She was still somewhat wary, reluctant to discuss her past—waiting, he knew, to be freed of her promise to Matt Preston. But the energy of her lightning onstage presence slowly took hold, reflected in her silvery eyes and in the emotions she seemed more willing to let herself feel. And there was vulnerability in the tentative touch of a woman newly in love yet still tied to her past.

But he was too fascinated by the emerging portrait of his love to worry about pasts.

They spent the day together, tacitly avoiding the other guests. They saddled up a couple of horses and rode into the mountains, taking a picnic lunch with them. Saber led him to her favorite spot overlooking the valley, a perfect place for lunch and privacy—and they took advantage of both.

Happier than she could ever remember being in her life, Saber was nonetheless a bit hesitant. She was finding the present a joy and a wonder, but the past disturbed her, and the future . . . the future was something she didn't dare dream of.

Travis seemed content and she had no doubt of his love, but would that love survive life in a goldfish bowl? In spite of his journalistic instincts, his interest in other lives, he himself was a very private man. And he had made no promises as to their future. She knew he was waiting for her to confide her past to him—but then what? Even if he could accept that past, understand it, would it color their future?

Would it always color their future?

She gazed down at Travis's sleeping face, her hands stroking the dark head that lay heavily in her lap. The horses, unsaddled, stood tethered nearby, drowsy in the cool shade; food had been consumed, remains packed away. The forest was quiet; Saber could hear only the rustling of leaves in the gentle breeze.

She looked at his unaware face, relaxed in sleep. Could he ever realize, she wondered, just how much larger than life he really was? His sensitivity and understanding still astonished her. Would any other man have waited so patiently for answers she knew he longed for? And taught her so much about love while he waited?

Her heart ached as she let herself think of what she would lose if he walked away. She looked at him and thought, *You're the life I might have had.* If it were simple, if they were only two people who loved...

But it wasn't simple. There were debts and

promises. There were circumstances neither of them could control. He had chosen for himself a relatively secluded but successful life; and, as a result, it was his work rather than himself that received public attention. If he decided to ignore public demands forever, neither his work nor his life would be seriously affected.

But her work...was performing for the public. She stood in a spotlight, pouring out her heart to an audience.

That could change, of course. She had wanted only success, never fame, and she had earned both. Was public performing necessary to her now? Was it a part of her life she could put behind her?

Were there still songs she wanted to sing?

Saber thought that she could sing now for an audience of one and be more than content. But was that what Travis wanted of her? She would not ask until he knew the truth.

She wasn't certain she would be able to ask then.

"Don't," he murmured huskily.

Saber had to clear her throat before she could speak. "Don't what?"

"Look sad." He sat up, turning to face her. His hands caught hers and carried each to his lips. "You seemed so . . . lost. I've never seen you look that way before. What were you thinking?"

Saber gazed into tender green eyes and tried to swallow the lump in her throat. "I was thinking that I live in a fishbowl."

"Does that bother you so much?"

"Yes."

He was quiet for a moment. "You have an incredible talent, Saber, but you have a life as well. An admiring world can't live that life for you. You have to choose. Live in a fishbowl where the world can see you—or don't."

She smiled wistfully. "You make it sound so simple."

"Isn't it? Isn't it really?"

"I could stop performing," she said steadily. "But could I ever get out of the fishbowl?"

"Take yourself out. Live in my world, darling." He hesitated, then went on quietly, "I would never ask you to give up a life you enjoyed, a life you needed. I wouldn't...I'd never take you away from the world just so you could be mine alone, so only I could hear your voice. But if you don't want that life"—his voice deepened—"then share mine, Saber."

"Travis—"

He lifted his hand, gently covering her lips with a finger. "I know there are things you feel I have to be told. And I know you won't commit yourself to me until that happens. But there's something you have to know, Saber. Whatever it is, it doesn't *matter*. It won't change anything."

"How can you be sure?" she whispered.

"Because nothing you could tell me would make me stop loving you," he replied softly, and his smile went straight to her heart. "In case I haven't mentioned it before, lady, what I feel for you is forever."

"Without knowing what's gone before?"

"Without knowing. I love you today, and I'll love you for the rest of my life."

Shaken, she reached out to touch his face with

trembling hands. "I don't think I deserve you," she murmured.

His eyes darkened, a flickering radiance in their emerald depths. "Saber, don't you realize what you mean to me? All my life I've looked for you, hungered for you. You were the dream I almost lost faith in. I felt half-alive until you. An observer. Analytical and uninvolved. When I saw you on that stage . . . like every other man in the audience, I wanted to go out and slay dragons for you. Then you came into the wings and looked up at me with wary silver eyes . . . and the dragons were nothing. I would have fought the devil in perdition's flames for your love," he finished almost savagely.

Gazing into the ferocious tenderness of his eyes, Saber felt the breath catch in her throat. Past and future were both forgotten in a rush of emotion, a surge of need.

"I love you, Travis," she whispered, going into his arms. "I love you so much!"

Gently, he pressed her down to the blanket as his lips rained kisses over her face, her throat. His hand slipped beneath the loosened tail of her blouse to stroke her side, her stomach. "You're so beautiful," he said. "So strong and warm...my Saber..."

"Love me," she murmured, her arms locked fiercely around his neck. "You're the only reality I can hold...Travis..."

Seeking lips fused together with hot, sweet need, tongues dueling for a victory neither would claim. Clothing was tossed aside carelessly, blindly, until the dappled shade dressed their bodies in nature's colors. The soft breeze caressed them silkily, warmly.

Saber pushed suddenly against his shoulder as they both took ragged breaths, rolling with him until she lay half across his hard body. Passion swelled within her, a driving need to express emotions too deep for words, too basic for thought.

Her fingers raked gently through the soft, curling hair on his chest, her lips finding a flat nipple that hardened instantly at her touch. She felt more than heard the groan rumble from deep in his chest, and his excitement heightened her own. Her hands explored hard planes and angles, muscled curves; her tongue searched and teased enticingly.

Travis cupped the nape of her neck, his fingers tangled in her long hair. Every sense tunneled, focused only on her touch. He was dimly aware of his heart pounding out of control, of the hot tremors jolting through him like an electric current gone wild. Mesmerized, he felt the lightning that was Saber galvanize his body, his mind, his soul.

He gasped when her lips followed the arrowing trail of black hair down over his stomach, her fingers lingering to trace his ribs. He sought to keep his aching, restless body still, muscles contracting involuntarily wherever she touched him.

"You are so wonderful," she murmured against the quivering flesh of his stomach. Her hands shaped his narrow hips lovingly, as if she were molding him in clay or committing him to memory in her heart. She gloried in the faint salt taste of him, the rough, erotic brush of hair against her lips. She could feel the increasingly desperate need in his faint, jerky movements.

Travis lost his breath in a hoarse cry when her caresses became a warm and tender intimacy; the sorcery of her touch inflamed him. He groped wildly for control and found none, his body responding to her as though time itself had ordained it, commanded it.

"Saber!"

She didn't resist when he drew her impatiently into his arms. And her simmering desire ignited at his first hungry touch. The pull of his mouth at her breast wrung a moan from her, and his hands held her body still when she needed so badly to move. She threaded her fingers through his thick hair and held him, an ache growing in her until it rose to block her throat.

"Travis," she choked out.

"My love," he said hoarsely, lifting his head at last to gaze down at her with feverish eyes. "You're so sweet. You're driving me out of my mind! Love me, Saber...love me...."

She felt what little breath she could command rush from her body as he entered it, felt the throbbing need of him filling the aching emptiness within her. Instantly her body cradled his, holding him with the deepest part of herself until his eyes burned with surprise and excitement and a groan was torn from his throat.

Strength and power surged within them both, the current lancing taut muscles and quivering senses. Hunger drove them desperately, bodies crying out for release. They moved together with one mind, one rhythm, each leading and following, driving and driven.

Saber felt her body spiral upward, felt the quickened tempo, the breathless rush of all her senses. At last the tension exploded and she cried out in a primitive triumph, holding him fiercely, loving him with every part of a body gone wild. Travis stiffened and shuddered, a groan rasping from his throat as his own body hurtled over the edge into oblivious pleasure. . . .

It was a long time before either could move. They lay close together as heated flesh cooled and breathing slowed gradually.

Travis raised himself up on an elbow, gazing at her relaxed, smiling face with wonder. "You go to my head," he told her. "You're the only bottled lightning I get drunk on...gloriously drunk. I lose myself in you, darling."

She traced a tender finger along his jaw, laughter dancing in her eyes. "I must be a very...apt pupil, then?" she asked solemnly. "I've learned how to please you?"

"*Please* me?" A grin tugged at his lips. "My darling love, if you pleased me any more, somebody'd have to lock me away. In case you didn't notice, I was about one breath away from insanity a few minutes ago. And I didn't teach you a thing—you were born knowing how to please me."

"Ummm." She smiled. "I've got a feeling you definitely *learned* how to please me," she said dryly.

He was still smiling, but his eyes darkened with a hint of worry. "I won't deny some experience. Does that bother you?"

Saber laughed softly. "No, darling, the women

in your past don't bother me. Now, one in your *future*—"

"Only you." He kissed her. "Once a man gets drunk on bottled lightning," he murmured, "anything else'd taste like water." Suddenly his eyes were vivid, full. "That's the first time you've called me darling."

She linked her arms around his neck. "D'you object?" she asked.

"No. Oh, no, sweetheart, I don't object." He kissed her again, then sighed. "You do go to my head. I haven't been thinking clearly since we met, and I've never thought to ask ..."

Perhaps because she'd been dreaming of what it would be like to carry his baby, Saber understood what he was trying to say. Smiling ruefully, she replied, "I haven't exactly been thinking clearly, either. But I'm all for planned parenthood and, as it happens, I—well, I made a promise on that subject. I'll be ... *very* surprised if we're surprised by a little stranger."

Travis didn't ask about that promise. He wanted to but didn't. She'd tell him when she could. His smile turned a bit wistful. "Do you want kids? Someday?"

Saber took a deep breath and let it out slowly, only just realizing that her answer came straight from the heart. "A houseful."

"Really?"

"Really."

He grinned. "Good. Me, too. Of course. I'm not too sure about the number you've apparently got in mind. At my advanced age—"

Politely, she said, "Your advanced age didn't seem to be standing in your way a little while ago."

"It didn't, did it?" he said, encouraged. "Like I said, darling—you *do* go to my head."

"Something does, anyway," she murmured. "And we're both ignoring time. Darling, I hate to end these pagan rites, but the sun's going down. Shouldn't we get decently dressed and head back?"

NINE

As they were riding up to one of the three barns sometime later, Travis suddenly exclaimed, "Good heavens—we *have* been ignoring time. Me especially."

"What've you forgotten?" she asked in amusement as she swung easily down from her horse.

Travis followed suit and gave her a wry look as they handed the reins to a stablehand. "The world. But specifically, I forgot that I promised to spend this coming weekend in California with the parents. I'll have to call them."

"You don't have to—"

"I know." He caught her hand as they headed up the path toward the main cluster of buildings. "I don't have to stay here with you. Is that it?" When she nodded, he said, "Darling, I'm staying with you as long as you'll have me. And if you make up your mind *not* to have me anytime in the next forty or fifty years, I'll just change your mind."

"Final word, huh?" She was laughing.

"You're stuck with me; face the facts like a good girl."

"Yes, sir."

Cory nearly ran them down at that moment, and her lovely face was a study in mock astonishment. "Well, *there* you are! And I thought somebody'd killed you and buried the bodies." Hands on hips, she surveyed them thoroughly. "And I'm not so sure they didn't. Hi, I'm Cory Stewart! I own the place, and I don't think I know you two."

"Very funny," Saber said, smiling.

Cory sighed theatrically. "I'm always the last to know." As she passed them to continue down the path, she added conspiratorially to Travis, "Glad to see you were able to fill in those blanks. Bye now!"

Travis stared at his lady. "Is it written on our faces or what?" he asked plaintively.

"Cory *always* knows," Saber told him. "And what was that about filling in the blanks?"

"When she gave me the advice I wanted to hear, she used that term to mean, um—"

"Never mind. I get the point."

"I thought you would." He grinned at her as they halted at a fork in the path.

Saber ignored the grin. "You'll have to make your call at the main house. Why don't you go ahead and do that?"

"And what'll you be doing?" he asked politely.

"I," she said, equally polite, "will be wandering around somewhere." Then she smiled. "I'll probably be back at the cottage by the time you are. If not, look for me in the clubhouse. I feel like playing the piano for a while."

"All right, darling." He bent to kiss her briefly but thoroughly. "Don't forget me."

"I'll try not to. If I do, though, you can always remind me."

"I'm looking forward to that." He leered and swatted her gently on the bottom as she turned away.

"Travis."

"I'm going, I'm going."

Alone, Saber strolled down the path, smiling. As she neared the building casually called the clubhouse, her steps quickened. Like every building at The Hideaway, it was unlocked, and deserted this time of day; the staff didn't normally man the place until around dinnertime.

She entered the shadowy interior, threading her way among the tables, past the bar and dance floor. Absently, she noted that Cory had recently redecorated, replacing beige carpet and mountain scenery prints with rich red carpet and wall hangings. The room was dim, lit only with soft bar lights; the small bandstand was completely dark.

Saber felt her way to the light switch and turned on the light directly over the baby grand piano. She moved to the bench and sat down, flexing and limbering her fingers. Ignoring the sheet music, she played a few classical bits, switching idly from one to another. Gradually, though, an unfamiliar tune began to come to life beneath her light touch.

She wasn't surprised by that; her best songs had come into the world in relaxed, reflective moments. After the crash, and when she'd known she would survive, many songs had played in her head. Luckily, her memory for music and words was excellent; those very songs had taken her to the top.

Now, still idly, she located the pencil and paper always kept on top of the piano. Her slender fingers sounded a few tentative notes on the keys, then repeated them thoughtfully. Words echoed in her mind, but she wanted the music down first. Leaning forward, she began putting the notes on paper.

Travis made more than one call. His feeling of security in Saber's love had strengthened until he felt certain that Matt Preston was not important enough to threaten their love. And, having realized that, Travis recognized that where Preston had been important was in Saber's *past.*

He sat for a long time in the main house, frowning, fitting together pieces of the last several days. He thought of two histories: one he knew completely because it was a matter of public record, and one that was a blank.

A blank...

A secret.

A secret.

Quickly, convinced he had it, Travis made another call, this one to his researcher "source." Because the man had had no contact with Travis since he'd first considered doing a book on Saber, he'd continued to work at uncovering her past. He hadn't found much...but he had found something.

Travis finished his call, then strolled back down the path toward their cottage. He looked in, found the place deserted, and made his way along another path toward the clubhouse.

And heard the music.

Unwilling to disturb Saber, he slipped quietly

through the door and moved among the tables until he was near enough to see her clearly without her awareness. He sat down, listening to the music rippling through the room, watching the lovely, absorbed face bent over the keys.

He didn't realize at first that she was composing. Then she stopped playing, picked up a pencil, and began to write on the paper in front of her. He listened intently as she began playing again. She went through one particular series of notes several times, frowning slightly. Then her face cleared and she played it again, changing several notes.

About fifteen minutes later, she played the entire piece through, and it was beautiful. Unlike most of the songs he'd heard her perform onstage, this music was soft and gentle. The tempo was slower, the rhythm quiet and understated.

Then she began to sing.

Enthralled, Travis listened to a Saber he'd never heard before. The power and passion of her stage presence were there; the startling ability to conjure emotion in the heart of any listener was there. But this gentle, husky voice was not meant to be flung out to an audience of thousands.

It was meant for only one to hear.

He felt a lump rise in his throat as tears stung his eyes. She might have been a siren or a mermaid voicing a sweet song to enchant the slumbering beast in a man. Or lightning arching brilliantly across a night sky. Or a woman quietly baring her heart.

It was a song of a love so deeply felt that the simple words were heart-wrenching. There was tenderness and sweetness and aching desire. There was joyous longing for the future. There was compassion for those less fortunate in finding such a love.

Travis rubbed at his eyes when the spotlighted picture of his love began to blur, and it was then that he noticed another had joined the audience.

Matt Preston stood in the doorway, his eyes fixed on Saber. He held the door partly open, and the light from outside clearly illuminated the older man's face.

Travis wanted to feel anger at the intrusion. He

wanted to leap to his feet and challenge the older man's right to hear emotions meant for himself. He wanted to let loose the primitive, possessive beast in the heart of every man, and cry *"Mine!"*

But he felt no anger. He watched Matt Preston's face, and what he saw there was a sad resignation.

Loss.

The billionaire gazed at Saber, his hard face softened, his cold blue eyes blurred with emotion. He stood and took the obvious pain and grief of hearing her gentle voice sing of love for another man.

He took it silently. Gracefully.

And Travis couldn't hate that kind of man.

He turned his gaze back to Saber, unwilling to intrude further on the older man's anguish. He felt no sense of triumph that he had won Saber's heart, only a deep sense of gratitude.

She could have had any man she wanted.

Travis hoped that he would one day learn to accept loss and defeat with the grace of Matt Preston. The man had been tortured with loss, and he stood silently accepting yet another. His eyes told of an open wound within him, but the pain and grief could be understood only by another man who had lost a dream.

Travis understood because he had found a dream.

And he knew then, in that moment, what it would have done to him if he had found Saber only to lose her.

It would have destroyed him.

Saber's sweet voice faded into silence, but her fingers continued to move over the keys. There was a distant, dreamy smile curving her lips, and her expression was tender.

The face of a woman in love.

Travis didn't bother to wipe his eyes. He turned his head slowly, finding Matt Preston still standing by the door.

The older man didn't wipe his eyes, either.

But he turned his head slowly, as if it hurt, until his blurred gaze found Travis sitting in the dimness. And from the misty blue eyes came something Travis heard as if it were spoken aloud.

So you're the one.

You're the one who's taken her from me.

You're the one who won.

And Travis could feel no anger. *I'm sorry.*

For a moment, Preston dropped his eyes to the large manila envelope in his hands, his mouth twisting in a sudden grimace. Then he tucked the envelope under an arm and turned. As silent as he had come, he was gone.

Travis sat where he was for a long time.

Roused from her dreamy abstraction by some vague realization of passing time, Saber finally stopped playing. She rose from the bench and gathered up the pages of her song, folding them carefully and sliding them into the pocket of her jeans.

She knew that it was a very good song. Recorded and released, it would likely sell millions.

But it would never be recorded.

This song was for Travis.

She hesitated, then pulled the sheets from her pocket and unfolded them on top of the piano. Reaching for the pencil, she neatly lettered a title across the top of the first page. Then, smiling to herself, she tossed the pencil aside and tucked the sheets back into her pocket.

Maybe one day she'd sing it to him.

She stepped down from the bandstand and took several steps toward the door before she realized she wasn't alone. Travis rose from one of the tables to move toward her in the dimness.

Suddenly shy, she wondered how long he had been there. What had he heard? What had he thought? When he finally stood before her, she knew the answers.

"Travis..." She reached up to touch his wet cheek, her heart turning over.

Silently Travis gathered her into his arms, holding her with the almost savage force of a man grasping the dream of his lifetime.

Saber slid her arms around his lean waist, holding him almost as tightly, her cheek resting against his chest. She could feel his heart thudding, feel the uneven rise and fall of his breathing. A wave of love and tenderness washed over her, tangled inextricably with astonishment and wonder.

What smiling fortune had granted her the inestimable gift of this man's powerful love?

After a long moment, they turned with one mind toward the door. She kept her arm around his waist, just as his remained around her shoulders. They walked together silently, following the path that would take them to their cottage.

When they were nearly there, Cory came striding up the path toward them. She halted abruptly, her lovely face still for a moment. Then, very softly, she said, "If I never see it again, at least I've seen it once." She dashed a hand across her brimming eyes, adding in a weakly irritated voice, "And I *don't cry,* dammit!"

"Cory?" Saber asked, worried.

"Nothing. It's nothing." She smiled brilliantly, but the green of her eyes held stark envy. "I'll have your dinner sent to the cottage, okay? I—I have a feeling you two want to be alone."

"Thank you, Cory," Travis said in a quiet voice.

Saber added, "Cory . . . if I had three wishes—"

"I know." Cory gave them another brilliant smile. "You'd wish for me what you have. Well, keep the positive thoughts, will you, friend? What you two have...doesn't come along very often." Quickly she passed them on the path, running her hand across her eyes with another irritated mutter.

They went into their cottage.

The next few hours were a time of quiet sharing. They touched almost constantly with a need deeper than passion. Their eyes met and held, silent vows exchanged.

They took a leisurely shower together and dressed, she in her comfortable caftan and he in slacks and a shirt left unbuttoned. Then they cuddled on the couch with wine on the coffee table before them and soft music on the radio.

And they talked quietly.

"Cory deserves love," Saber said, looking at her own man. "She's helped so many people."

After a moment, Travis smiled. "Maybe it's our turn to help Cory."

"How?"

"Ever tried your hand at matchmaking?"

"She'd kill us."

"She doesn't have to know about it," he countered innocently.

Lying half across his lap, Saber laughed. "True. D'you have anybody special in mind?"

"As a matter of fact, yes. And if he doesn't fall head over heels in love with Cory at first sight, I haven't known him for the last ten years."

"But will she love him?"

Travis considered briefly. "Well, I've never looked at him from a woman's point of view, you understand."

"But?"

"But I'd say he had the devil's own charm. And when he wants something, he goes after it single-mindedly."

"Is he a paragon like you?"

Travis grinned. "Nobody's a paragon like me, darling! But to answer your question, I'd say . . . he was a warlock."

"As in magic?"

"Uh-huh. Think Cory can handle him?"

"The question is, can he handle Cory!"

"My vote's on Jake."

"This," Saber said reflectively, "should be interesting. When could you get him up here? Cory's not about to leave The Hideaway until her book's at least a year off the bestseller list."

"Ummm. I'll have to find out what he's doing at the moment. It may not be easy to get him away from his work for a vacation."

"What does he do?"

"He's a prince."

Saber stared at him. "I beg your pardon?"

"You heard me."

"A prince? As in blue blood and royalty?"

"That's him."

"A prince named Jake?"

"His mother's American, and she liked the name. What can I tell you?"

"Prince of a *country*?"

Travis laughed. "Like most of today's royalty, sweetheart, Jake's is more or less an honorary title. His father is Italian, and the title was handed down from the days when it meant something, unlike many Italian princes, however, Jake's father had the foresight to do some canny investing. The family's quite wealthy now, and Jake has interests in a shipping firm and an airline—not to mention several offshore oil rigs."

A bit dazed, Saber said, "What's his last name?"

"Sebastian."

"Prince Jake Sebastian?" She shook her head bemusedly. "He sounds a very strange sort of prince."

"Looks a strange sort of prince, too. Like a mountain, in fact. There must have been many tall Americans in his mother's ancestry."

"This is the man you're going to sic on Cory?"

"Please, darling. I'd never *sic* him on her. I'll just tell him about this great place I know where he can relax and unwind. And if that doesn't work," Travis added thoughtfully, "I'll hire somebody to kidnap him."

"How did you come to meet him?"

"We met in college. He was terrific in math and I was great in English; it was instant friendship."

Saber thought about it for a moment, then giggled. "Assuming your matchmaking works out, does that mean Cory would be Princess Cory?"

"That's what it means."

"Good heavens."

"I like it."

"You would."

He started laughing. "It's perfect, darling. Cory's got to be the most queenly-looking lady I've ever seen in my life. If anybody could carry off the title of princess—however honorary—it's Cory. She'll stand Europe's elite on its collective ear."

Before Saber could respond, a knock at the door announced the arrival of one of The Hideaway's cheerful waiters with their dinner.

"Just call the main house when you want this stuff taken away," he advised them when everything was set out on the table, then left as quickly and efficiently as he'd come.

Cory had even sent candles.

They enjoyed the meal, talking occasionally but not needing conversation to fill the time. When the leisurely meal was finished, they called and had everything taken back to the main house.

Alone again, they were just about to get comfortable on the couch when Travis bent to pick up the folded sheet music from the coffee table. He looked at Saber. "May I?"

She smiled at him and sat down. "Of course."

Travis unfolded the sheets and gazed at them for a long moment. The words were branded on his heart, unforgettable, and it was the title he stared at. Slowly, he began to smile. " 'Larger than Life,' " he said.

"I thought it was ... apt."

He placed the song back on the table and came to sit beside her. He slid an arm around her, drawing her close. "I love you," he murmured, kissing her gently.

Saber smiled up at him, a touch of wonder in her eyes. "I love you, too. I ... I never expected you, you know."

"You didn't dream of Prince Charming?" he chided gently. "I thought every little girl did that, just as every little boy dreamed of finding a princess and slaying a few dragons."

"Did you?"

"Certainly. Maybe it was that little boy who first recognized his princess standing onstage under a spotlight."

She continued to smile, but her silvery eyes dimmed in memory. "I don't think I ever dreamed of a prince. Not the way most little girls would, I mean. I didn't dream of fairy castles or a...rescuing love on a white horse."

"What did you dream of?" he asked.

"I dreamed of a house with a white picket fence," she said wistfully, still lost in memory. "Of roses growing in the yard, and a weeping-willow tree by a stream in back. I dreamed of a little mongrel dog and a scruffy cat. Of comfortable furniture and needlepoint pillows tossed casually around. The sounds of laughter from lots of children." She laughed softly. "Leaning over the fence to talk to the mailman. Driving to get groceries in a station wagon. Collecting coupons and green stamps.

"And I dreamed of...being held in the night. Jokes too private to share. Laughter and love."

Travis hugged her silently.

She looked at him, the tears in her eyes clearing slowly. "Very...mundane dreams, huh? No fairy castles. No dragons. Not even a prince."

He cleared his throat. "No, not mundane, darling. Just your version of...happily ever after. Is that the life you want now?"

"It's the life I never thought I could have."

"And now?"

Saber sighed. "Now? Now I want it even more."

"Your music?"

She no longer believed Travis would walk out of her life when he learned the truth, but it was always possible. The future, the plans she hardly dared let herself dream about...would they actually become reality? Ruthlessly, she banished the past from her mind. It wouldn't change anything. *It wouldn't!*

"My music," she said slowly, "was always meant for me. A way of expressing myself. An outlet for hurts and dreams and fears. I don't think I'd ever want to stop singing. But I also don't think"— she looked at him, her heart in her eyes—"that I need an audience anymore. I don't think I need a stage or a spotlight to hide behind. I think ... I can sing in a garden ... or in the shower ..."

"Or to me?" he asked huskily.

"Or to you. Especially to you."

He touched her face with his free hand. "I'd love to hear you singing in a garden or the shower—or to me. But would the short career you've had this past year really satisfy you, darling? Will you feel cheated someday?"

Saber smiled at him. "If I had found that dream of mine sooner, there never would have been a career, and I never would have missed it. Now that I've had it, I'll miss it even less."

"The world will miss it."

"Will they?" she asked wistfully, still smiling. "Darling, in spite of what you think of my talent, you have to remember that the career of a popular singer is usually as short—and as brilliant—as a falling star."

"Not yours," he replied firmly. "You can be famous as long as you want to be. You've got the talent to shake the world."

She was a bit shaken herself. "But I don't want

that, Travis. I want to live with you and grow roses
and babies...."

He gathered her into his arms. "As long as
you're sure," he whispered unsteadily into her soft
hair. "I couldn't bear it if you woke up one day and
felt cheated. D'you understand that, darling? I
want you with me for the rest of our lives, in a
house with a white picket fence. I want to watch
our roses and babies grow and bloom. I want that
dream with you!"

Saber held on to him because he was that
dream, and she had never wanted anything so
much in her life. "I won't feel cheated," she whispered. "With you beside me, I'll never feel
cheated."

"Then it won't be a dream! We'll live it!" he told
her fiercely.

"I hope so," she murmured, the past prodding
her suddenly. "I hope we can."

Travis lifted his head and looked down at her,
frowning a little. But before he could speak, a
knock sounded at their door. Trying to bring a
smile to her sober face, he groused softly,

"Wouldn't you know we'd have company just when I want you to myself."

He was rewarded by her smile and kissed her quickly before rising and heading for the door, which he swung open with the intention of getting rid of their visitor fast.

Matt Preston stood there, looking at Travis with his unreadable blue eyes. They were much the same in height, and both were powerful through the shoulders, narrow at the waist. They stared at one another in silence for a long moment.

Then Travis stepped back and gestured for the older man to enter. It wasn't what he wanted to do, but he knew that Preston brought with him Saber's past, and that it was time for them to face it.

Preston said nothing until the door was closed behind him and Travis had moved to stand with unconscious protectiveness near Saber's shoulder; she was on her feet and gazing steadily at the older man.

But he didn't return her stare. Instead, he looked at Travis, his expression still inscrutable. "You trust her," he said. "Without knowing, you trust her."

"I trust her," Travis replied evenly.

Preston nodded as though some private deduction had been confirmed. Then he looked at Saber. In one hand, he held a large manila envelope. "And you trust him."

"Yes."

He held out the envelope to her.

Without looking, Saber took it and tore it neatly in half before handing it back to him.

Preston looked down at the torn envelope, his mouth twisting a little. "I thought you'd do that. Funny—I didn't read it, either."

Saber looked quickly at the envelope and saw that the flap was still sealed. Then her eyes lifted to Preston's. "Why?"

"Because ... because I heard you sing. I got the report and went looking for you, and you were singing. I knew then that whatever was in this envelope wouldn't matter ... to either of us."

"I told you it wouldn't."

He nodded. "Yes, you did. And I knew then that

I'd lost you. I just didn't want to admit it to myself."

She reached out quickly to touch his arm but
said nothing.

The older man took a sighing breath, then nodded. Silently, he turned on his heel and left the cottage, closing the door behind him.

Quietly, Travis said, "He's your father."

TEN

Saber turned to stare at him. After a moment, she smiled. "You guessed. I thought you would."

"I guessed. When I could think clearly, I realized it was the only thing that made sense." Curious, he added, "What was the report about?"

"You," she answered as she sat down on the couch. "From the day you were born until now, it contained everything Matt's investigators could find about you."

"Why?" He sat down beside her, knowing the answer.

"He was trying to protect me," she said.

"Protect you from me?"

"You. Anyone who could hurt me." Saber sighed softly, searching for words. He knew, but it was important—so important—that he *understand*. "Have you ever watched a magician work, Travis?"

He frowned. "Yes. So?"

"Sleight of hand. Legerdemain. To make an illusion convincing, the magician creates a plausible diversion; the audience is so busy watching the diversion that they never see the trick." She sighed. "Matt Preston created a diversion years ago, Travis."

"A son," he murmured.

She nodded. "A son born and raised in secret. A nameless, faceless son, secure in his anonymity." She smiled, a twisted smile that had alerted Travis unconsciously. "Matt pulled the trick of the century . . . and he got away with it. The secret son was so diverting that no one ever thought to look for a daughter."

Travis sighed. "I knew about Preston's past because I'd researched it," he said. "And you were just the right age. Then, when I thought of the blankness of your past . . . it fit. It all fit."

"After losing his first two children and his wife to tragedy, he wasn't about to lose me. So Matt directed everyone's attention to a fictitious son, and while the press scrambled to find that son, he was able to watch his daughter grow."

"But—all these years," Travis protested. "There was never the least hint."

"Matt spent a fortune," she said dryly. "And he has the ability to win intense loyalty from friends and employees. You were right when you guessed I'd attended school outside this country. A succession of schools—under assumed names. Select, expensive schools, where children of the very rich were hidden away like the precious offspring of a rare breed. I had a number of fictitious backgrounds, all ultimately untraceable—like most of the other kids I went to school with."

"Then you didn't see much of...of your father?"

"More than you'd think, given the secrecy. There was always an aunt or uncle—employees or friends of Matt's—to come for me at vacation or holidays, a jet to whisk me away to wherever he happened to be. He was reclusive in his personal life; security was everywhere." Again the twisted smile. "Many of the 'friends' of my childhood wore coats specially cut to hide the guns they carried to protect me; I thought of them as uncles. Alex, for instance, has known me all my life."

"You poor kid," Travis said.

Saber laughed softly. "Oh, I was a princess. Guarded, pampered, spoiled. Always the best of everything. And Matt loved me; I never doubted that. He loved me so much he spent twenty-six years pretending to the world that I never existed."

She gazed into distance and memory. "It wasn't easy for him. I could never even call him by anything but his name for fear someone would hear and guess the truth. And he was terrified of losing me the way he'd lost everyone else who mattered to him. When I was small, every upset stomach or cold threw him into a blind panic. He worried about accidents, about kidnapping if my identity became known. And when I was older ... well, there were other worries."

Travis knew now why Saber hadn't dreamed of castles and princes. She had led what most would have considered a fairy-tale existence; what Saber had hungered for had been a quiet, gentle reality.

He cleared his throat. "What other worries?"

"Men. Whether I wanted it or not, I stood to inherit an empire. That's quite an inducement for an ambitious man. Matt was afraid I'd be taken advantage of, that I was too ... innocent and easily hurt."

"And you were," Travis murmured, remembering the studio photo of a delicate, gentle face.

"Once I was." She looked at him intently. "I was nineteen when I thought I fell in love. I was at school in Switzerland. I told Matt how I felt, because I'd promised him I'd never tell anyone who I was without his approval. He flew over a couple of days later—with a report." Saber shook her head.

"And the report was too complete to be denied. It seemed that this man I thought I loved had tried more than once to marry money. He didn't know who I was, but he knew *what* I was."

"What happened?"

"Another school. Another name."

"No." Travis reached to take her hand, gazing at her steadily. "What happened?"

She knew what he was asking. "I cried. Oh, not for that shallow man, or for the loss of him. I cried because...until then, I hadn't known what Matt was protecting me from."

"Saber..."

She gestured slightly, pleadingly, needing to tell it all now and, if possible, put the past behind her. Travis nodded.

"I don't want you to think I wasn't happy. I was, for the most part. Especially when I could be with Matt. But the only thing I ever wanted was the one thing Matt could never give me."

"A normal life?"

Saber nodded. "Matt's kind of notoriety is a very rare thing. I could put a year of fame behind me because there's nothing as dead as old news and yesterday's legends. But Matt...he's a *world-mover.* If he spent the remainder of his days in total seclusion, the world wouldn't forget. Wouldn't leave him alone. He learned to live with that. But in the end, I couldn't."

"Life in a fishbowl." Travis shook his head. "But it wasn't really that for you, was it?"

For a moment, she was silent; then she sighed. "No. It was the world in a fishbowl, and I was outside it. It was so hard to find an identity for myself. No name, no past I could claim. *Who* I was...was so much bigger than *what* I was—and yet who I was, I couldn't claim. I was so confused for such a long time. I could—could have raised an army to guard me with a word, but I couldn't point to a speck on the map and say, 'That's home.'"

He squeezed her hand. "Was that when you decided on a career?"

"Yes. I never wanted fame, Travis. I just wanted to...to take care of myself. To make some small mark on the world as myself—not Matt Preston's daughter."

"He couldn't have been happy about that."

She laughed hollowly. "No. Oh, no. He wasn't a bit happy." Then her face tightened. "I knew what I was doing to him. And for me to choose a career as a *singer* ... up onstage in front of people, unprotected. Crazies taking shots at anyone with a claim to celebrity. We argued for months." She paused. "I'd never argued with him before."

"And he let you go."

"Yes, he let me go. He would have wrapped me in cotton wool if I'd let him, but he knew I wouldn't. The only thing I'd let him do for me was to fabricate yet another fictional background."

"Saber Duncan was born."

"Yes. He insisted on providing a checking account and charge cards until I was on my feet. And we agreed that I'd never tell anyone who I was." She sighed. "I even agreed on birth control, because he was still so worried that someone would take advantage of me. Then I went out on my own." She smiled ruefully. "And failed."

"Those first two records?"

"Horrible, weren't they?"

"No," he corrected gently. "Just not strong."

"Failures. I . . . I couldn't deal with that. So I ran. I didn't want Matt to know how upset I was; I decided to create the fiction of a vacation, and call him when I got there."

"Where?"

"New Zealand."

"Where you crashed?"

Saber nodded. "I was feeling a bit reckless. I knew one of Matt's jets made a weekly run to New Zealand, so I sneaked aboard and convinced the pilots—both of whom I knew—to let me hitch a ride. They were longtime employees of Matt's, and they knew who I was. So they kept quiet about a passenger, and took off on their regular run."

"He must have gone out of his mind when you disappeared."

"I—Yes, he did. And the worst part for him was that he had to search quietly and secretly. He didn't dare publicize my disappearance for fear that I'd become even more of a target. When the report of the crash came in, and the pilots' bodies were found, no one could have guessed I'd been on board. There was no clue to my whereabouts. He had to carry on as if nothing were wrong, while he mobilized a secret army to find me."

"Did they find you?"

"Oh, yes. Without thinking, I used a credit card to buy some clothes and a backpack. Alex was waiting for me at the airport in Auckland."

"You hadn't called your father?"

"Funny—Alex made some comment about that. No, I hadn't called him. Cruel of me, I know." She looked at Travis steadily. "You know what I went through after the crash. I felt like I was a different person. I think a part of me knew Matt would grieve for the girl I could never be again. It was a second loss I was to blame for. I turned away from the life he wanted to give me, and then I destroyed the gentle girl that reminded him so much of my mother."

"You grew," Travis argued softly. "You changed. It was inevitable, Saber. He must have known that."

"Yes. But it didn't make things easier."

"Was he the one who was unnerved by the lightning?"

She smiled a little and nodded. "I could see that it bothered him. And it seemed to bother other people, too."

"So you hid it, except onstage."

Saber nodded again, watching him with an expression torn between hope and dread.

Travis smiled slowly at her. "Was all this supposed to make a difference to me, darling?"

"It...it very well could have. Travis. I don't want the empire my father built. But it could be mine one day. I hope not, but it's possible. Unless and until that happens, I won't be acknowledged as Matt's daughter and heir. He won't make me a target. But you must realize that could change. Somewhere down the road, we could find ourselves the focus of a worldwide spotlight."

"I assume," he said dryly, "you expected me to take to my heels?"

She couldn't help but smile at his expression. "Well, not recently. But I have thought that maybe..."

Travis gazed at her for a long moment. "Tell me something, love. Why didn't you read your father's report?"

Saber was surprised. "Because I love you, and trust you. Whatever it said wouldn't—" She broke off abruptly.

"Change how you felt?"

She nodded.

"Yet you thought your past might change how I felt?"

"Well..."

"I should turn you over my knee," he said severely.

"I was afraid," she admitted.

His green eyes sparkled as he laughed at her; then, without warning, he sobered. "I love you, Saber. And right now my major emotion is relief because Matt Preston is your father rather than the rival who's been haunting my nightmares."

"I thought you might have been considering something along those lines," she murmured.

"You did, did you?"

"It was rather obvious. I *told* you I wasn't in love with him."

"And then immediately said that you loved him."

"I couldn't explain, Travis."

"I knew that, darling. And then a little later, I overheard you talking to your father."

Saber looked at him blankly, then nodded. "In front of the cottage. Just before you—"

"That straw broke the camel," he murmured.

"You were afraid I'd been Matt's mistress?"

Travis thought about it. "Earlier it had crossed my mind—when I first met him out by the pool. Later, I was certain that wasn't the relationship, but I knew he was important to you, a part of your past."

"You never guessed he could have been my father?"

"Not until today. All my fine analytical instincts were on holiday as far as you were concerned. Moments before I realized Preston knew you, my brain had drawn its own logical conclusion as to his missing 'son.' "

"And that was?"

"Mark."

After a startled moment, Saber giggled. *"Mark?"*

"Well, dammit, it could have fit. He's the right age, and he and your father both have blue eyes. In addition to that, I decided that it was possible Preston was still concealing his son's identity *because* that son was Mark; he certainly wouldn't fit into the business world. It seemed logical that Preston would keep quiet to allow Mark a life of his own."

Saber laughed quietly. "I can see how you might have jumped to that conclusion. We've both known Mark about eight years—since he started coming up here from time to time. He fascinates Matt; all that talent wrapped in a blanket of vagueness, but with flashes of shrewdness. I doubt if Mark has even realized that Matt could be the world's best patron for a young artist: he just enjoys their conversations and loves to paint Matt. He says Matt has a face like Charlemagne."

"You mean the face of a king?"

"It's what Mark means, I gather."

"He's right."

She laughed again. "How ridiculous it all is! I couldn't tell you anything; since you'd slated Mark for Matt's son, it never occurred to you until today that *I* could be that 'son'; Matt was worried about a journalistic writer interested in my past—"

"Was that what bothered him the most?" Travis nodded as he thought it through. "Yes, I could see how it would."

"That's why he came up here," she murmured.

Startled, he said, "*Why* he came? You mean he expected to find me here?"

"Not exactly." Saber smiled slightly. "Matt's been keeping a very close eye on me, Travis. You went through my manager to arrange a meeting with me. Now, I don't know who it is, but somebody on Phil's staff is Matt's employee—there for the express purpose of keeping Matt informed of possible problems. Such as . . . curious journalistic writers."

"I see."

"Yes. Well, Matt was tipped that you were inter-

ested in doing a biography on me. He knew I'd refuse, but he also knew your work and reputation.
He called the hotel—remember?—to find out for
sure where I'd be going on vacation. Then he
arranged to spend a few days up here, intending to
discuss with me just how much of a threat you
might be."

Travis grimaced. "And promptly met me by the
pool."

"Uh-huh."

"He has quite a poker face," Travis noted ad-
miringly. "He was so charming I never guessed I
might have been a threat to him."

Saber giggled a little. "Yes, well—like another
tiger I know, his charm is one of his most dangerous assets."

"I'll take that as a compliment."

"I thought you would."

"I'm going to ignore that," Travis informed her
regally. "Go on with the story, please, ma'am."

"Well, Matt instantly requested his people to
gather a report on you. He decided that if you were

serious enough to follow me up here, you were quite definitely a threat."

Travis frowned a little, thinking. "I see that. But . . . I remember now that when he asked Cory if she'd told you he was here, he seemed almost to expect that his arrival would anger you."

"Was that when you wondered if I were his mistress?" she asked, interested.

"It crossed my mind, and can we drop that, please?"

She giggled. "Certainly. Well, to answer your implied question: Yes, Matt expected me to be angry, because his presence here proved he had a spy on Phil's staff and was therefore keeping a closer eye on me than I liked. He knew I'd be mad, and I was."

Travis nodded, amazed at how a fleeting expression on a man's face could be so innocent and understandable with the right explanation, where before it had been a threat. "So what he was worried about was my exposing your identity."

"Right. He didn't realize then that there was any . . . personal involvement."

Curious, Travis asked, "If there hadn't been, and I'd been interested only in a story, determined to find out who you were, what would he have done?"

"Thrown dust in your face," she answered promptly. "He wouldn't have tried to buy you off or—in spite of some colorful accusations from the supermarket rags—have you killed. He simply would have laid a false trail for you to follow."

"And I would have followed it?"

Saber smiled. "No slur on your abilities intended, darling, but Matt's been hiding me for twenty-six years, and some pretty tough investigators have given the problem their all. He could have provided me with an innocent, foolproof identity that you would never have suspected was fabricated."

"I suspected the Saber Duncan 'life,' " he pointed out.

"Yes, but that was never intended to stand up to close scrutiny. Matt's a magician, but false trails take time. Even as you were digging into my fictional background, Matt's people were working to fill in the gaps; nobody expected me to succeed as quickly as I did, and we were all caught off balance by the sudden interest in me."

"But he has the false trail ready now?"

"Nearly ready. Saber Duncan will soon have an identity even the most suspicious will be unable to disprove."

"Won't that make it impossible for you to claim your inheritance if you have to?"

"No. Everything I need to prove I'm Matt's daughter is hidden away in a bank vault that rivals Fort Knox for security. And if, by chance, something happens to that information, three of Matt's most trusted friends have duplicate information hidden away with equal security. All are under orders to find me instantly if anything happens to Matt."

Suddenly Travis chuckled. "Forgive me, darling, but it sounds like something out of a spy novel!"

Seeing the humor of her situation, Saber laughed as well. "I know. Isn't it ridiculous? As you can see, Matt is *very* careful!"

"Just protecting the gem of his life," Travis said. "I can understand that—now."

"I understand it, too. But it's hard sometimes. On me and on him."

Thoughtful now, Travis said, "You've been everything to him. All that was left of his wife. . . . I gather he adored her?"

Saber's face softened. "Yes," she said quietly. "Yes, he did. She was a frail woman physically, and the tragedies of losing her first two children nearly broke her. The doctors had warned her against getting pregnant again so soon, but—but she wanted a child so badly. She *needed* a child." Saber sighed, then smiled slightly. "Matt never blamed me for her death. I was told later—by Alex, who was there—that Matt went berserk when my mother died. When he picked up his child, even the doctor was afraid for me. But Alex said he held me for hours: he said everyone who knew was convinced that if I had died, too, Matt would have gone insane."

Travis reached for her hand and squeezed it gently. Seeking to ease her sadness, he said quietly, "So you were everything to him. No wonder it hit him so hard to come up here and find—"

"And find me in love with a journalistic writer," she finished, eyes lightening a bit.

"A double threat."

"Yes. Matt's a good judge of character, and he formed a favorable impression of you when you met. But he still couldn't help considering the possibility that you might be determined to expose a twenty-six-year-old secret."

"And . . . you loved me," Travis added.

"And I loved you. He's known for some time that I couldn't live his life, that I hated security and secrecy. But I was still his child. And he was still the only man in my life. Until you."

Travis nodded slowly. "That's hard for any father to accept. A strange man in his daughter's life, in her heart. Even worse for him. Any man could wreck your life with a careless word, and your father knew it. He had to protect you as far as he could, and cope with his own sense of loss."

"He said that he heard me sing the song. Did you see him?"

"I saw him." Travis smiled at the memory. "I wanted to hate him, Saber. When I first saw him there, listening, I wanted to hate him. It seemed to me that he was intruding. But then I saw the grief and resignation on his face. The loss. I didn't think of a father losing his daughter to another man, but of a man losing a dream to another man. And I couldn't hate him because . . . because I knew how I'd feel if I lost you. And because he was accepting his loss with more grace than I'll ever have."

Saber held his hand tightly. "Don't be too sure about that," she said. "You have more grace than you realize."

Travis shook his head but said nothing. "I hope your father and I can be friends one day."

"You will be."

"Does he realize I want to marry you?"

A demure smile curved Saber's lips. "Well, he asked me about that, but since you'd never *said* in so many words . . ."

"I never said?" He was astonished.

"Never," she said firmly.

"We talked about children."

"Yes."

"And a house with a white picket fence."

"We did."

"And sharing our dream."

"I remember."

He furrowed his brow in a mock frown. "But not marriage?"

"Never marriage."

"Not a word?"

"Not a single word." Saber frowned back at him. "And it'd be a bit much for you to take me away from Matt only to turn me into a kept woman. He wouldn't like that at all."

"I imagine he wouldn't." Travis said feelingly.

She smothered a giggle. "But of course, since you've never *asked* ..."

Travis caught her suddenly in his arms, eyes laughing but intense. "Then I will. My beautiful bottled lightning, will you marry me?"

Saber, too, was abruptly serious. "It really doesn't bother you, Travis? Who I am, I mean?"

"All I want," he said steadily, "is you beside me for the rest of our lives. If your father's ... empire...intrudes in the future, then we'll deal with it in the future."

Slowly she slid her arms around his neck, eyes shining up at him like stars. "I love you," she whispered, "and I'll marry you tomorrow if you like."

"That might...just...be soon enough," he murmured, kissing her.

He lifted her up as he rose to his feet, and she asked teasingly, "Another storm coming?"

"Can't you hear it?" He padded steadily toward the bedroom door. "Wind and lightning—force ten, at least. We'll have to batten down the hatches, darling."

"Ummm. I just love storms...."

"By the way," Travis murmured a long time later. "What *is* your name?"

Curled up at his side, she laughed softly. "Preston."

"I know that." Gently he swatted a rounded hip.

"Oh, you mean my *other* name."

He hugged her. "Stop being difficult, woman!"

She laughed again. "My name is Saber."

"What?"

"When I decided to live my own life, I also decided to claim my own name—part of it, anyway. Saber Preston is the name I was born with."

Travis rubbed his chin against her soft hair. "I love you, Saber Preston. With all my heart."

Saber lifted her head to smile at him, tears shimmering in her silvery eyes. "That just...might... be enough."

ELEVEN

THOUGH BLOOD TESTS generally take time, a doctor friend of Cory's in Prescott rushed theirs; Saber and Travis were married two days later.

The situation couldn't have been better under the circumstances. The marriage of two such celebrities would have generated instant public attention almost anywhere in the country—except at The Hideaway, where more than one match had been quietly and discreetly formalized. Neither Saber nor Travis could have hoped to escape public notice completely; an announcement would be made later, with the location of the ceremony remaining secret.

It was felt by the principals that the second announcement they would make would quite divert attention from the first: the announcement of Saber's retirement from public performance.

"Are you *sure* that's what you want, Saber?"

"Quite sure, darling."

"You won't miss it?"

"No. But you might get tired of my singing in the shower."

"Never. . . ."

Though no one had planned it, the situation was also best for Matt Preston. It would have been difficult, if not impossible, for him to have been present for his daughter's wedding had it taken place anywhere else. It was not known that he was at The Hideaway, and since he tended to disappear periodically, not even the most suspicious would ever connect his current "disappearance" with a quiet wedding that took place at the same time.

The ever-efficient Cory located a minister who

wouldn't have known a celebrity if he'd fallen over one and had no earthly idea that he was marrying two of them and had been introduced to a world-famous billionaire.... Cory also arranged for an adoring records clerk to handle the license without ever noticing that he could have made a small fortune in bribes—either to talk or to keep his mouth shut.

The other guests never knew that a wedding had taken place practically beneath their noses; Cory arranged a special party to keep everyone occupied, and no one even saw the reverend.

So, while the guests enjoyed their party, Saber and Travis were quietly married beneath a large tree, on the edge of a meadow, with Matt to give his daughter away and Cory, Mark, and Alex as witnesses. Mark happily sketched the ceremony, then presented the pictures to them as his present. Birds provided the only music, and the wildflowers Saber carried filled the air with sweetness.

The rings they exchanged had been chosen and purchased in Prescott the day before in a tiny jewelry store too far off the beaten path to attract celebrities; the jeweler saw only a glowing couple fathoms deep in love and looked no further than that.

Saber wore a beautiful old-fashioned ivory wedding gown that was one of Cory's many contributions to the couple's future happiness.

"It was my mother's; she was a half-pint like you. God knows *I'll* never be able to wear it!"

Also courtesy of Cory was the tuxedo Travis wore.

"Darling, you have to hurry and get that prince up here. Cory *deserves* a prince."

"I'll see what I can do. . . ."

The knot was well and truly tied.

Since neither could think of a place better than Cory's retreat for their honeymoon, there they remained. And if the other guests noticed the gleaming new rings worn by the couple they had watched fall in love, no one commented. It was a tacit rule at The Hideaway to "forget" whom or what one had seen, and that rule was upheld by the guests, all of whom yearned for at least one private retreat where they could rest and relax.

Though he did not intrude on their privacy, Matt Preston also remained at The Hideaway. And because of the kind of man he was, resignation inevitably gave way to acceptance, which in turn blossomed into happiness at his daughter's obvious joy.

But the wary businessman who had learned caution during a hard and tragic life could hardly help but succumb to suspicion when his newly married daughter joined him and Mark in the main dining room one night barely two weeks after the ceremony.

"Where's Travis?" he asked as Saber sat down across from him.

Saber, whose eyes resembled stars these days, sent him a quick smile. "There was something he had to do."

"Will he be joining us later?"

"No," Saber answered casually. "Cory flew him down to Prescott this morning. He'll be back in a couple of days."

"Will he get my paints?" Mark looked up from his plate to ask.

"Of course he will, Mark. He promised, didn't he?"

Quietly, Matt asked, "He's staying in Prescott?"

Saber looked at her father, knowing that only time would allay the concern she saw in his eyes. "I don't think so."

"Then where?"

"I didn't ask, Matt."

"You have a right—"

"Matt." She smiled at him. "I haven't known Travis very long, but I know him very well."

Her father sighed. "I know you trust him, honey, but..."

"But?"

Reluctantly, Matt said, "A man could live out his life in luxury for the price of...a secret."

Saber wasn't angry. Her father had gone through a great deal in his life, and she knew it too well to be angered by his doubts. "Do you honestly—*honestly*—believe Travis would do that?"

"No. I'd be very surprised if he did. But I've been mistaken in men before."

"Not this time."

"I hope not, honey. But if you don't know where he is..."

"I know where he isn't. He isn't selling a secret to the highest bidder. And he isn't holed up somewhere in a hotel room writing about the 'lost heir.' "

Neither of them worried about talking in front of Mark. If he guessed the relationship between them, which was entirely possible, he would never reveal his knowledge by a careless—or knowing—remark. For all his amiable vagueness, he was honest and loyal. And they were both his friends.

"Then where is he?"

Saber smiled. "He had something to take care of."

Matt looked at her thoughtfully. "Testing your faith, perhaps?"

"No, Matt, he isn't testing my faith. I can assure you, he didn't *want* to leave." Her eyes turned inward, remembering and savoring their tender good-bye. Then she focused on her father's face. "It's something he had to do."

They ate in silence for a few moments, then Matt said, "Would he have gone to tell his parents?"

"No, we're going to do that together. *And* explain the reason behind all the secrecy."

Matt frowned slightly.

"They have a right to know," she said.

"Yes. I know."

Abruptly, they heard Mark's soft, hurried voice:

"If there were dreams to sell,
  What would you buy?
Some cost a passing bell;
  Some a light sigh,
That shakes from Life's fresh crown
Only a roseleaf down.
If there were dreams to sell,
Merry and sad to tell,
And the crier rung the bell,
  What would you buy?"

As his companions stared at him, he added helpfully, "Beddoes. I think," and returned his attention to his plate.

"I have no idea what you mean," Saber told the artist.

"Buying dreams," Mark said vaguely. "Nice if you can do it. Some people can. Some can't. Some dreams aren't for sale." Then, before Saber could ask for further clarification, the artist excused himself and left the table.

Matt unerringly recaptured the subject uppermost in his mind. "Saber, I could—"

"No," she interrupted, "you couldn't. Matt," she added in a softer voice, "please learn to trust Travis. Whatever he's doing, it's for me. For us."

"How do you know that?"

"The look in his eyes when he asked me to ask no questions," she replied.

After a moment, Matt nodded. Then, slowly, he said, "You want no part of my empire, do you, honey?"

"You know I don't. I respect what you've built, Matt. But I've made plenty of money in my own right, and so has Travis. He'll write because he's a writer, and I'll sing to him and our children."

He nodded again. "I don't see how we can avoid

eventual public disclosure," he said. "You've a right to claim the name you were born with, and your children will deserve to know their heritage."

"Yes," she agreed quietly. She knew by her father's expression that this was something he had thought out at some length.

"Then"—he smiled, the mischievous smile of a canny magician about to produce a rabbit—"maybe we can turn this famous secret of ours into no more than a nine days' wonder."

"I'm for that. How?"

"I'll disinherit you," he said promptly.

She couldn't help but giggle. "That sounds easy enough. But will it work?"

"It will," he said, "if I start dismantling the empire immediately."

Saber was more than a little startled. "Matt, you don't have to do that."

He laughed quietly. "Honey, I'm not doing this just for you. I've spent the better part of my life making money—and now's the time to spend it where it'll do the most good." Soberly, he added, "There are causes crying out for support. Financial backing. And the days of empires are past; no one man should have the power I have."

It was serious remarks like that, Saber thought lovingly, that made her father so special. Because he *meant* it. "It'll be quite a task," she pointed out, "even for you. All the companies, the properties, the investments."

"It'll have to be done carefully," he agreed. "If I dumped all my stock on the market, I could easily knock the bottom out."

"Years," she murmured. "It'll take years, won't it?"

"Oh, easily." Suddenly he grinned. "I've already laid the groundwork with the lawyers, so it'll be done even if I don't live to finish it."

Saber was smiling at him. "So I'll end up being just the daughter of a mad ex-billionaire?"

"Something like that. We'll delay the disclosure of your identity until we can time it nicely. If I know the press and public—and I do—the initial attention over you will gradually be pushed off the front pages." Seriously, he added, "You may have to hire some kind of security for the duration, but

I'll make damned sure you won't be anything near the target you might have been."

Softly, she said, "Thank you, Daddy."

The blue eyes that had unnerved kings and presidents brightened with a sudden sheen of tears.

"You never asked much of me," he said huskily. "Just the chance to live your own life. And . . . it's so good to see you happy."

Saber reached out to hold his large hand. "I want you to be happy, too."

"I am, honey. I have a busy time ahead of me—and a chance to set a few people on their ears! More than anything, though, I feel at ease about your future for the first time."

"In spite of doubts about Travis?" she teased.

"Do me a favor," he requested wryly, "and don't mention that to him. That's a formidable man you've married."

Saber giggled. "You two should form a mutual admiration society. He practically thinks you hung the stars!"

It was just the right note, and their laughter rang out from contented hearts.

"Travis?"

"Don't peek!"

"Travis, where're we going?" Saber nearly had to shout in spite of the headset, because the helicopter was making the usual noise and, in addition, the blindfold her husband had insisted on was covering her ears as well as her eyes. "Travis?"

"Not much longer now," he said soothingly.

"I know what it is," she told him with mock gloom. "You're selling me to a white slaver." Always at ease in helicopters, Saber was nonetheless glad that Cory was at the controls; being blindfolded made the ride quite disconcerting.

She had no earthly idea what Travis had told her father, but scant hours after her husband had returned to The Hideaway, Matt had seen them off with a wide smile and laughter in his eyes.

Cory, too, had been merry, her green eyes brilliant with humor. And something else. Saber couldn't forget that "something else," because it was the same starkly envying expression with which she had regarded the love of her friends.

What in heaven's name was Travis up to?

His voice reached her ears now.

"Selling you? My darling love, only a fool would sell the most precious gift to ever come his way."

His voice was cheerful, but the words were tender, and Saber felt a slight blush rise to her cheeks, aware that Cory had heard every word.

"Blarney!" she managed to say. "You're trading me in on a new model after only two weeks and three days!"

"Later," he told her firmly, "I'll demand an apology for these base accusations."

"Where are we going?"

He laughed close to her ear, and Saber felt a warm shiver course through her body. The effect this man had on her was nearly indecent. . . .

Saber felt her ears pop and thought that they were either dropping or climbing; it was difficult to be sure. They had been in the helicopter for what seemed a very long time, but passing minutes were as difficult for her to gauge as altitude. But they did set down once briefly to refuel, which told her they were quite a distance from The Hideaway.

Were they even in Arizona?

Sometime later, Saber felt the aircraft touch ground. Before she could speak, Travis was cheerfully ordering her to stay put. After a few moments, with the helicopter still making its normal racket, the door on her side opened, her headset was removed, and she herself was lifted easily in Travis's arms.

"Thanks, Cory!" Travis called.

"Don't mention it," she shouted back.

The helicopter lifted away with a rumbling roar.

As Travis carried her across what appeared to be uneven ground, Saber tried to guess where they were. Mountain air...and quite an altitude, she thought.

"I hope you appreciate the trust I'm placing in you," she told him severely.

His chuckle sounded rich and warm in the still air. "Oh, I do, love."

"If you don't tell me where we are—"

Interrupting her, he spoke casually. "We've never really talked about where we should live. I doubt that your apartment in L.A. or mine in New York would be quite what we'd like. D'you agree?"

"Um ... yes."

"I think we want a certain amount of seclusion—don't you?"

"Well, a certain amount."

"Right. Close enough to a town so the kids can go to a good public school."

Saber cleared her throat hesitantly. "Uh-huh."

"And where neither of us is likely to be bothered by nosey reporters."

"That's for sure."

"And room for everything. A big house. Yard. Maybe a bit of land so we could have horses. Would you like horses?"

"Yes." Saber caught an elusive scent and tried to identify it. Was it—?

She was set gently on her feet as Travis halted, her back turned to him. His hands held her shoulders lightly, and she could feel the broad strength of his chest behind her.

"It's bright up here," he murmured. "Better keep your eyes closed at first." Then he lifted the blindfold away.

Cautiously, Saber opened her eyes. And the breath caught in her throat.

"It needs some work," Travis said softly. "Inside and out. Paint and paper, carpet. And the roses haven't been pruned in years."

She barely heard him, too enthralled by the reality of an old and dear dream. *"If dreams were for sale, what would you buy?"* Now she knew what Mark had meant.

It was a large, rambling house; an old, comfortable house. The white clapboard needed paint and there was a shutter askew. Rooms had been added throughout what must have been a long life, until the house spread out with little grace but with a welcoming, endearing air. A covered porch ran the length of two sides, and the windows were the large, many-paned kind that would collect dust easily but would sparkle when clean.

The house stood at one end of a lovely mountain valley; there was rolling pasture in the distance, heartbreakingly green. A long graveled drive wound its way toward a distant road, which in turn meandered lazily toward a small town.

Large, graceful trees shaded part of the yard; the grass was a bit overgrown, but as green as the pasture. And there were half a dozen rosebushes, in need of pruning and care, but gloriously in bloom.

And around the yard was a white picket fence, as in need of fresh paint as the house, but standing sturdily for all of that.

"How . . . how did you find it?" she whispered.

Travis held her gently against him. "I came up here to visit a friend a few months ago. He was building a house nearer to town, but said he didn't want to sell this place—except to someone special. He's the one I left The Hideaway to see. I've got the key, so we can go inside. There isn't much furniture, but enough for us if you want to stay a while." Hesitantly, Travis added, "If you like it, we can sign the papers in a few days."

"If I like it?" She turned in his arms, lifting a face aglow from within. "Travis—it's perfect!"

His own face lit up. "I hoped you'd think so," he said huskily. "We'll have the acreage for horses, and there are half a dozen bedrooms."

"Let's go inside," she said eagerly.

"Don't you care where we are?" he asked, amused.

Softly, she answered, "We're home."

Travis held her close. Then, as they turned toward the house, he suddenly said, "I've been meaning to ask you, sweetheart—what's your definition of a hero?"

Saber looked up at him, surprised that he didn't know. Gently, lovingly, she said, "A hero is a man who can hold the lightning . . . and not be burned."

ABOUT THE AUTHOR

KAY HOOPER is the award-winning author of *Blood Sins, Blood Dreams, Sleeping with Fear, Hunting Fear, Chill of Fear, Touching Evil, Whisper of Evil, Sense of Evil, Once a Thief, Always a Thief,* the Shadows trilogy, and other novels. She lives in North Carolina, where she is at work on her next book.

Don't miss the second thrilling novel in
Kay Hooper's Blood trilogy...

Now on sale from Bantam Books